THUNDER IN THE HILLS

THUNDER IN THE HILLS

SUSAN MEADMORE

COMPASS PRESS
* OXFORD * MELBOURNE *

First published in 1981 by Robert Hale Limited

Compass Press Large Print Book Series; an imprint of
ISIS Publishing Ltd, Great Britain, and Bolinda Press, Australia
Published in Large Print 2002 by ISIS Publishing Ltd,
7 Centremead, Osney Mead, Oxford OX2 0ES,
and Bolinda Publishing Pty Ltd,
17 Mohr Street, Tullamarine, Victoria 3043
by arrangement with the author c/o Mary Irvine

British Library Cataloguing in Publication Data
Meadmore, Susan,
 Thunder in the hills –
 Large print ed.
 1. Large type books
 I. Title
 II. Sallis, Susan
 823.9′14 (F)

Australian Cataloguing in Publication Data
Meadmore, Susan.
 Thunder in the hills/
 Susan Sallis, writing as
 Susan Meadmore.
 1. Large print books
 2. Love stories
 I. Title
 823.914

ISBN 0–7531–6634–8 (hb) ISBN 0–7531–6635–6 (pb)
(ISIS Publishing Ltd)
ISBN 1–74030–632–5 (hb) ISBN 1–74030–677–5 (pb)
(Bolinda Publishing Pty Ltd)

Printed and bound by Antony Rowe, Chippenham and Reading

F

CHAPTER
ONE

Trains were arriving from London every hour and we met each one until ten o'clock.

Dad worked on the railway in the control office and he said it was terrible at Paddington. He said people were fighting to get on trains to escape the bombs. He said Florrie was far too timid and gentle for that sort of thing; she'd go back home and try tomorrow, so we might just as well do the same thing. Mum knew differently. Florrie was her sister so she knew her pretty well. Mum said Florrie would get on a train somehow because of Philippa.

Dad, trailing down to the platform from the office — he was on the late turn — said wearily, "Better for Philippa to stay in London and take her chance."

Mum glanced at me sidelong. "I suppose you'd say the same if it was our Lily."

Dad said, "Lily's got something to give the world. Philippa's a mongol. All she can do is take."

Mum didn't argue about that, which showed she agreed with Dad. She always argued if she'd got a fraction of a case. She was dark and thin and sometimes fierce-looking like a starling. Dad was dark, too, but plump and slower and he scoffed at everything. The Royal Family, old Hitler, our vicar, the Labour party. Everything. It got Mum on the raw often.

She dropped the subject of Philippa and said stubbornly, "Our Florrie'll get on a train. I know her. She always gets what she wants."

"Even Bert," Dad said dryly.

Bert was Florrie's husband. Uncle Bert. Met on Southend Pier in 1926 and married just before Philippa arrived in 1927. Uncle Bert was blond and beautiful and glorious fun. How I loved him.

"Why isn't he coming to stay with us?" I pestered, bouncing my gas mask against Dad's legs to get attention. "Why can't Uncle Bert come? I can sleep with Philippa and he and Aunt Flo can —"

"Why indeed?" Dad looked at Mum, but she wouldn't meet his eyes.

She said, "He's away just now, Lil. One of his traveling jobs."

Another train came in and people poured from it. It was only three hours from London but they looked as if they'd traveled for days. The women's hair was coarse and stuck up from their stiff bobs. The kids were pale yellow. The luggage seemed to be mostly teddy bears, dolls, cat baskets, and of course gas masks strung in their cardboard boxes around the shoulders and necks like mascots.

They coagulated around the ticket barrier and we waited there, Mum on tiptoe to spot Aunty Florrie's raven head, Dad solid and officially scornful behind her, and me — already knowing they weren't coming — staring at my sandals, which after a summer of tough wear had the homely personalized look of all my favorite clothes. Winter lace-ups never got that look. Sandals were special. Sandals were destined to travel through brooks and up trees and into very special places among our fields and woods. Sandals were part of the joy of summer.

Dad said, "Well, that's it. There won't be anything else tonight. She's been sensible for once and waited till the first mad rush is over."

Mum, frustrated and baffled, hung on till the bitter end, which was a couple of wheelchairs. The occupants looked half dead. Surely they would have preferred Hitler's bombs to the indignity of flight?

"It's not like our Florrie," Mum muttered as we got into the Austin with the magic number GY 4396 and the horn that sounded like a skein of wild geese. "It's not like her at all. On her own up there with Philippa. I thought the first thing she'd do would be to get down to us. I doubt if Bert left her any money —"

Dad ground the gears horribly and I smoothed the shiny leather of the seat in silent sympathy with GY.

He said irritably, "So that's the real reason she's coming, is it? What a bit of luck Adolf walked into Poland yesterday. It gets Florrie out of a nasty hole. Hey what?" When Dad wanted to say something nasty he often tempered it with a jocular "Hey what?" It didn't allay Mum's immediate fury.

"Look here, Albert Freeman. I've put up with your cantankerous father all these years and now I want to give shelter to my sister and her poor child for a few months until this ridiculous war is over and you start on! If it weren't for Florrie and Phil we'd be lumbered with half a dozen evacuees, I might remind you! That billeting officer from the Shire Hall said it was only because Philippa is . . . like she is . . . that he'd leave us for a while. We've got room for two other children besides them. How would you like that? Hey what?" She really was mad. Her head, turned toward Dad, sleek blue-black hair bouncing on her neck, made stabbing movements as if for two pins she could have bitten into his bland cheek. I put one sandal up on the seat and let my fingers explore the cutout diamond pattern of them in the musty car darkness.

Dad said cheerfully, "I wouldn't like it at all, my dear. But it wouldn't be *me* putting up with it, would it?"

Mum conceded that point and changed her tactics.

"It will be wonderful for me to have a bit of congenial company . . . stuck out there by myself all day . . ."

This was Mum's chorus and was in the nature of an armed truce. We bumped over the level crossing and the tall thin houses of Georgian Gloucester leaned down, friendly dark silhouettes against the summer night sky. A flash of white marble — the War Memorial from the Kaiser's War — then

Stroud Road. I slept and thought of the raft we were making and the new teacher . . . a man . . . Mr. Edwards. The texture of my sandals, gritty with stubble raspings, reminded me of the corn dollies Nanny Dexter made with her arthritic fingers. Like tapestry my wonderful, carefree life rolled behind my eyes. I was happy but didn't know it because I'd never been anything else. Like a small animal, I had my own territory in our part of the Cotswolds. In that territory I was perfectly free. Mum was a town girl, but her loneliness in the country made no demands on me. In fact it gave me another dimension because I was also at home in her part of Gloucester. And the bickering between her and Grandad . . . her and Dad . . . was nothing. It never included me. I was the beloved only child. Their mutterings were far above my head and like distant thunder they merely emphasized the warmth of the summer day.

I knew when we were there because the air changed quite suddenly from the pungent smell that hung around the Gloucester Gas and Coke Works to the first hint of the heavy harvest we were still gathering. People think of the Cotswolds as bare sheep hills, but in the folds there are apple orchards and cornfields and weighted plum trees and gemlike market gardens. And the bald sheep smelled good, too. Like Nanny Dexter. Musty and secure.

Dad switched off the engine and we rolled down the track to the house so as not to wake Grandad.

In the silence Mum's whisper reached my ears quite clearly.

"I thought you said you wouldn't be called up. I thought you said the railways were a reserved occupation." She still sounded mad and frustrated. Also frightened.

Dad was as light and cheerful as ever but not so scornful.

"You don't have to wait to be called up, Grace."

I forced myself to concentrate and grabbed my sandal buckle so it stuck into my finger.

"You wouldn't volunteer, Albert? You wouldn't leave me and Lil in this dump all by ourselves? Not even you could be that selfish?"

"Dad would look after things. It would be good for him. And it sounds as if the house is going to be packed out, what with Flo and —"

"Ah. Now we're at the real reason. You want to get away. Because Florrie's coming. Because I'm not the fun I used to be —"

We stopped and Mum opened her door and waited. But Dad didn't say a word. She got out and slammed the door and immediately a light went on in Grandad's bedroom. I scrambled over into her seat.

"What will you join, Dad?" I was so excited I could feel my insides fizzing. "Be an airman, Dad. Ron Morgan's dad is an airman and he's got a badge on his blazer like in his dad's cap and —"

Dad scooped me off the seat and held me against his shoulder. I couldn't breathe, he held me so tightly. After a bit he put me down.

"I'll be a bloody infantryman, Lil. That's me."
His voice was thick. I'll probably clean out the
privies and shine some officers' shoes and say yessir,
nosir . . . just like I do now. What the bloody hell am
I going to prove doing that?"

He didn't want an answer, but I searched my
mind and remembered last Armistice Day and the
teacher's sonorous voice just before the two minutes
of silence.

"You go to fight because you love your country,
Dad," I said in suitably solemn tones.

He snorted a laugh, then he couldn't stop.

Then he gasped, "Love my country, Lil? Don't
you believe it! I don't love anything very much." He
put his chin on my head so that I couldn't see his
eyes in the darkness. "Christ, Lil. I'm thirty-two and
I don't know what the bloody word means."

He got out of the car and carried me to the
house. I wanted to tell him what love meant. I
knew. Everyone knew. But somehow I couldn't
explain it.

Aunt Florrie arrived at three A.M. in a hearse-like
taxi, the front of her beautiful gray cloth coat caked
with Philippa's sick.

The hearse didn't bother to cut its engine, and in
any case Aunt Florrie's gasping screams at every
pothole woke us up in good time to realize what was
happening and get down the stairs to let them in. It
was as usual a terrific, flurrying, kissing, tearful
welcome.

"Darling. It was awful. Just awful. Lily, I do believe you've grown since July. Phil's freezing, Grace. Could you light the fire? Oh, darlings, it's so wonderful to see you. To get out of that death trap. It was hell in the train — everyone was sick and there was nothing to drink and we were so *thirsty*. I could *kill* Hitler."

Dad actually laughed. Mum took Florrie's coat and tutted over it admiringly. Philippa, her head hanging, held my hand and towered over me like a shy giraffe. Grandad grunted and shifted himself as far from her as he could in our little living room. He looked rather like a picture of an armadillo in my children's encyclopedia.

"How about me fare?" The taximan lugged in the last of the cases and stood blinking at Grandad while Mum nodded fiercely at Dad, and he fumbled for two half crowns in his pocket only to discover he was wearing his pajamas.

I looked up at Philippa and her big moon face looked back down at me. I started to laugh and she joined in and we couldn't stop; we rolled about like a pair of drunken dancers, laughing and laughing.

"What on earth's the matter with you?" Mum asked. And Grandad gave grunting advice about throwing cold water on us while Dad tipped the tea caddy out to find change.

"It's like the circus," I spluttered helplessly. "He's an owl —" I nodded surreptitiously toward the taxi driver. "You're a starling. Dad's a —" I couldn't call

8

Dad a clown in front of the others so I just keeled over against Philippa.

Aunt Flo was delighted.

"Lily can always make Phil laugh," she said, smiling and looking like Joan Crawford. "I'm glad we came. Lily is so good for Phil."

I wondered what she would have said if I'd told her that Philippa was the giraffe in the circus.

Phil and I sat on the mat in front of the sofa while the grown-ups listened to the news on the wireless. Poor Mr. Chamberlain sounded upset, but all that was happening was that ambassadors were coming home from here, there, and everywhere and we were told what to do if an air raid happened. There was a lot about Warsaw. I loved the name Warsaw and said it over and over to myself.

I whispered, "If it gets like Warsaw here, we can hide behind this sofa and shoot at the Jerries as they come down the track. We could hold them off for ages." I edged myself onto the sofa seat so that I could see out the window. The cushions would protect us from any bullets; nothing could get us if we were behind the sofa.

For the first time in all the talk and hullabaloo Phillipa looked frightened. She dribbled.

"Shooting hurts people," she said in her hoarse voice.

"Kills 'em," I told her nonchalantly. "That's what we've got to do. Kill all the Jerries stone-dead."

She whimpered, "No, Lil. No, Lil. No, Lil. No, Lil."

"Don't be daft." I pinched the back of her hand so she wouldn't start rocking. Everyone got upset when she rocked. "If we don't kill them they'll kill us."

She looked sick. No one had hurt Philippa in all her twelve years. Aunt Flo had seen to that.

I said, "Not you. I don't mean you, Phil. You'll be all right."

She brought her long neck forward, then back. "You, Lil. And Mum. Mum and Dad." Tears mixed with her dribble.

"That's why we got to get 'em first," I murmured, desperately trying to block her shoulders with mine. "Look, Phil. We can hide down like this — come on down here with me. Then when they come down the track — bang, bang —"

From behind us Grandad gave a terrific grunt, more like a pig than an armadillo.

"We ought never to have let 'em rearm in the first place!" he roared. "We ought to have shot the lot of them out of hand. Now the rotten buggers will swarm all over us — there's nothing to stop 'em —"

Philippa rocked violently and wailed like a banshee.

Aunt Florrie leapt up from the wireless and rushed to her.

"What have you been saying to her, Lily? Trust you to upset the poor child —"

Mum put a protective arm toward me. "Lil wouldn't do anything to hurt Philippa — you know that, Flo."

Philippa went on wailing and I had to raise my voice to be heard.

"I was only telling her about Warsaw and how we can hide behind the sofa and —"

Philippa screamed and Aunty Florrie turned a furious face to me.

"She doesn't know anything about the war, you little fool! She doesn't understand!"

But Philippa understood. Her tortured eyes, normally so mild, met mine, and I knew she understood better than any of us. And because of her understanding, it suddenly came to me what was happening. The trains coming from London full of people who were frightened. The Warsaw ghetto. Aunt Flo living with us. Dad going to join up.

War had come to the hills. My own territory.

I started to cry.

CHAPTER
TWO

The ice on Nanny Dexter's pond was the best for miles. Ron Morgan, Freda Willis, and me were the best sliders. Nan came out on two sticks and stood watching us and cackling when we fell down. Philippa laughed all the time. Sometimes she made a fierce attempt on her long giraffe legs to follow us and down she'd go, her arms flailing the air, the scarves and hoods Aunt Flo made for her tripping her up and winding her like a mummy.

"You big, daft nelly!" yelled Dennis Crake furiously when she got in his way. "Geroff, can't you?"

She just laughed again and ran over the crackly grass at the edge to where Nan waited for her. Ron did one of his special slides, turning all the way around and shoving Dennis into the petrified willows.

"Sorry, Den," he said casually.

I went to the far side of the pond, grateful to Ron for defending Phil for my sake, mad with her for making it necessary. Philippa promised to be a millstone.

Afterward we special few went into Nan's cottage for cocoa. She had plenty of milk and she put a spoonful of sugar in with the saccharin.

"Takes the bitter taste away, m'dears," she told us, stirring the enamel jug and looking witchlike through the steam. "And if you mixes a bit of that dried egg muck with the marg, it's more like butter, too." She darted us knowing looks. "Not that any of we are short of a bit of butter, eh?"

She wasn't talking black market. In the hills the old system of bartering had returned. For a few hours' potato planting or muckraking you were paid in milk and butter. But Nanny Dexter couldn't work anymore and I wondered what she had to barter.

It was Freda who put me wise.

"Wish it were tea, Nan." She gave one of her whispering giggles and nudged Ron. "Then you could read the leaves."

Nan darted her a look through the steam. "Tea's on ration, my girl, and don't you forget it." She poured carefully into enamel mugs. "'Sides . . . I don't need tea leaves to see things. Nor no crystal balls." She passed me a mug and looked at me very straight, and I wondered if Mum had ever said anything to her. Mum always slammed the door on the gypsies and never let me go into a fortune teller's tent at fetes. Once when Dad crossed someone's palm with silver for a laugh, Mum said with terrible logic, "If it's supernatural, it means it isn't natural. And if it isn't natural, it isn't right."

Nan went and stirred her fire. It was set in a rusty range at waist height, and in the enormous ash box beneath it she had a never ending supply of potatoes baking in their jackets. She lived almost entirely on these, topped with butter and cheese and plenty of salt. Sometimes there was rabbit stew, and in the summer she preserved fruit in stone jars and dipped a spoon in them at random. She never had a cold, and though arthritis twisted her joints, it didn't stop her making her corn dollies.

She said without boasting, "I told Farmer Crake his cow would drop twins. And her did. I always knows whether a woman be having a boy or a girl in the first month." She glanced at me again, holding her smoking poker like a wand over the flames. "I just knows, that's all. Nothing unnatural about that, is there?"

So I knew Mum had said something. And, of course, that was how Nan got her butter. And cheese. And spuds.

I swallowed. I couldn't bear anyone to criticize Mum even indirectly. When Dad did it sometimes I hated him. And this was a kind of criticism. Once when Audrey Mackless said Mum was a foreigner, I hit her and made her nose bleed. On the other hand Nan was special. Nan was a bit like my sandals in the summer.

I looked straight back at her.

"Tell us our fortunes then, Nan. Go on. Tell us. Do me first — do me and Phil together 'cos we're cousins."

She stayed still, her poker poised above the blazing fire, her hooded eyes unfathomable. Then suddenly she cackled.

"Not today, Lily. I don't use my second sight to amuse a gaggle of kids!" She stood the poker upright in the hearth and turned with difficulty to sit in her chair. Her liver-marked hand reached for my coat sleeve and she patted me. "You're not a bad girl, Lily. For all your wild ways. And what can you expect from a Freeman crossed with a Gloucester girl?"

Freda whispered a giggle. "You sound like a hybrid, Lil."

"Don't call me Lil," I snapped. But I wasn't ill-pleased. Crossbreeding interested me. Fascinating things came of it.

Ron was sipping his cocoa, his blue hands gradually thawing around the chipped enamel. He kept slipping a smile at Philippa. She was rocking but without agitation. She finished her cocoa and put the mug carefully into the hearth, then she reached for Ron's hand. My face flamed with shame.

Nan adjusted her hat — she wore the same hat summer and winter, in and out of doors. "You're all eleven this year, eh? Who's going to sit the scholarship, I wonder?"

I sipped noisily and wriggled about so no one would look at Phil.

"We all are, Nan. Mr. Edwards says we're the brightest class he's had for years. We can do our tables backward and we know all the countries in the Empire."

"He's got a Welsh accent," Freda said adoringly. "And he sings in the chapel choir. Lovely, it is." She sounded the image of Mr. Edwards the way she said that. I wished ardently he didn't go to Freda's chapel; it gave her such an unfair advantage.

I did my best. "He has a drink with Dad in the Plume of Feathers, and Dad says he's a man that can take his beer." It was very important in the hills to be able to take your beer. But the people who went to chapel didn't believe in drink.

Freda went pink. "I can tell you one person who won't be taking the scholarship, Nan." She giggled. "She isn't sitting a hundred miles away, and she's already thirteen so she's a bit old for it. And she's very closely related to Lil."

My face flamed again, and I didn't know what to do. Whether to pass it off with a laugh and feel I'd betrayed Philippa or whether to have a row and probably start her off wailing.

Ron grinned at Freda. "I ain't related to Lily — and I ain't no 'she' neither. How did you know I wasn't going in for the scholarship then, Freda? You chapel folk got your ears to the ground all the time, ain't you?"

Freda put her cup inside Philippa's and didn't meet Ron's calm gray eyes.

"I meant . . . her," she said. But the sting had gone, and she was the one looking foolish.

16

Ron went on grinning, and Nan cackled back at him. I realized he hadn't moved away from Philippa's hand. Maybe he had knocked Dennis Crake over for Philippa's sake, not for mine. It set me free. But it was a freedom I suddenly did not want.

At Christmas we went to the Air Raid Wardens' pantomime at the school hall. I couldn't remember such a cold winter and I reveled in the iron ground, the delicate iced filigree of the elm trees, the smooth white slopes of the higher Cotswolds all around us. It was my job to wipe Philippa's nose before it froze into a glacier, and I didn't mind even that. Another job was to change the big white plaques that read "Your firewatcher tonight lives here." Phil wasn't allowed to come with me for that, and I pretended I was a dispatch rider and zoomed through the village at a terrific rate. Sometimes I locked the plaque onto the wrong gate and got into trouble. I couldn't see it mattered because even on the occasional raid nobody bothered to watch for fires. At least Mum and Aunt Flo didn't when it was their turn.

By the time the pantomime started we were all in a good mood. Farmer Crake got us warmed up with singing "Underneath the spreading chestnut tree, Mister Chamberlain said to me, if you want to get your gas mask free, you must join the A.R.P." Then the curtains were jerked back and there was Dad and Mr. Willis as the two ugly sisters in Cinderella. Mum and we knew all Dad's lines backward so we laughed before the jokes came up, and Dad came to the front of the stage and said, "If the two ladies in hand-knitted pixie hoods would like to come and take our places, they are more than welcome." Everyone laughed — so did I — but Mum didn't. She shut her mouth tight and went pink. When it was time for the audience to sing the chorus at the end, no one raised more than a whisper and Dad came to the front of the stage again.

"As the aforementioned ladies know this song back to front and upside down, I would be grateful for their cooperation."

Everyone turned and looked at us again and Mum's mouth was tighter than ever. Then she whispered, "You're not besting me, Albert Freeman," and she dumped her bag in Aunt Flo's lap and grabbed my hand and we pushed past all the knees and climbed onto the stage. Her eyes flashed at Dad and she shouldered him aside on the stage and we started up a duet.

> We're going to hang out the washing on the Siegfried
>   Line.
> Is there any dirty washing, mother dear?
> We're going to hang out the washing on the Siegfried
>   Line
> If the Siegfried Line's still there . . .

Aunt Florrie's clear soprano chased after us and Phil's hoarse bass was there too, but everyone else trailed behind because Mum was a foreigner. I

18

glanced at Dad as he lounged in the wings, his smile well in place, and it was one of the times I hated him. I went to the very edge of the stage and yelled out, "Come on, everyone!" at the top of my voice. And at last they bellowed it out.

Whether the weather may be wet or fine
We will jog along without a care
We're going to hang out the washing . . .

Mum hugged me on the way back to our seats. She'd be all right so long as she had me. When Dad went in the army I'd look after her. I'd look after her always . . .

After the pantomime the cast came into the hall in their makeup and costumes and went on joking in character while they passed the lemonade and teacups. Mr. Morgan, home on leave, came over and talked to Grandad about the phony war, with Ron just behind Mr. Morgan like a proud shadow. Knowing Mr. Edwards was too busy to stop them, the evacuees wormed their way out of the scrum and began chasing around the rest of the school. Mum, Aunt Florrie, Phil, and me sat in a row; Mum and Aunt Florrie did a lot of laughing and drinking their tea with little fingers raised, Phil was smiling and content, and I made hideous faces at my friends receiving and giving semaphores and hissed messages above the clatter.

Mr. Edwards was talking to the Willises in the front row. Freda made sure I knew about it by waving me frantically and jabbing at his downbent curls. She had been a bridesmaid last summer and her mother had let her wear her long dress tonight. It was a slippery rose-colored satin with green velvet bows all down the front, and she had matching shoes, too, though I couldn't see them.

I said to Phil, "That's our teacher. Sandy curly hair. Talking to Freda Willis' mum and dad. He ought to have been in the pantomime tonight — he sings lovely — all Welshmen can sing lovely."

Phil stretched her neck still more, then retracted it, satisfied.

"Like Dad," she said gruffly. "Smiley. Like Dad."

I looked again. Yes, there was something a bit like Uncle Bert about Mr. Edwards. A certain warmth.

He straightened and said his farewells, then came down the aisle toward Mr. Morgan's uniformed figure.

"Good evening, ladies." He swept the four of us with his clear blue eyes and inclined his head so it looked like a bow. "Mr. Freeman senior, is it not?" Grandad grunted angrily. "And Mr. Morgan. Welcome home, sir."

Ron's smile nearly split his face in half. Mr. Edwards smiled back and touched the darned sweater, acknowledging Ron's pride.

Mr. Morgan still spoke in his Gloucestershire burr.

"Good of you to lend the school for tonight, Schoolmaster. Wouldn't have been so handylike at the village hall."

"It's a question of blackout," Mr. Edwards explained meticulously. "The Shire Hall let us have a certain amount of material — enough for this room at any rate — and so far the village hall committee haven't raised enough funds to —"

Ron jumped up and down. "Sir. Sir. The 'vacuees are switching on the lights in the infants' room. Jerry'll see us for miles."

"Take Dennis Crake and round them up for me. There's a good lad. No fighting, mind." Mr. Edwards glanced at me. "Will you go too, Lily? Perhaps a feminine touch —?"

Nothing was going to move me from Mr. Edwards. I shook my head, unable to speak, and slid my eyes in Philippa's direction so that Aunt Florrie couldn't see me. He glanced at Phil, then away, embarrassed.

"Ah. Yes. Well . . . I did want a word with you, Mr. Morgan, out of Ronald's hearing . . ." He was wearing gray flannel trousers and a very hairy jacket. The back of his hand was covered with flaxen hair and I would dearly have loved to brush my face against it.

"I understand that you are against Ronald going in for the scholarship. You know I have to put a list forward for the first part of the examination immediately after Christmas, and I would like his name to be on it."

Mr. Morgan tugged at his coarse blue uniform.

"'Slike this, Mr. Edwards, sir. My wife be long gone and Ron d'live with his grandparents while

21

I'm away. They'll need his help. 'Sides . . . Ron's a country boy. Not much chance of getting a place in a city school, would you say?"

Mum stiffened by my side and Mr. Edwards said firmly, "Every chance, I would say, Mr. Morgan. And Ronald . . . Ronald is one of the few boys who could make something of a good education. He has potential."

Mr. Morgan laughed. "He don't show much signs of it at home — always out in the fields instead of at his books. An' his figurin' is 'opeless —"

Mr. Edwards said quietly, "Ronald will learn. Wherever he chooses to be, he will learn from it. Please, Mr. Morgan."

"Oh. All right." Mr. Morgan shuffled, embarrassed at the schoolmaster pleading with him. Ron's dad had been our local hedger and ditcher, and no one had ever asked him a favor except to get out of the way. He could hardly wait for Hitler to get into Poland before he joined up. He went purple-red when Mr. Edwards shook him warmly by the hand and was glad to collapse in the vacant seat by Grandad as soon as he was released.

Mum cleared her throat. "Er . . . Mr. Edwards . . ." He was already moving away. I could have kissed her. "I wonder. Could I have a word with you about Lily's chances in the scholarship?" She had pushed back her pixie hood and the blue-black hair was sleek over her ears. With her color high and her dark eyes lit with something more than irritation, she was beautiful. She and Aunt Florrie were aristocrats among the villagers. I tried not to grin with pride like Ron, but now that Mr. Edwards had seen my mum and compared her with his chapel-singing Mrs. Willis, surely he would smile on me rather than Freda?

Mum was telling him that she had gone to the high school and so was anxious I should follow "in the maternal footsteps" — she laughed delightfully asking his indulgence. He gave it.

"Well now, Mrs. Freeman. Lily . . . yes. Perhaps if she works hard — really concentrates. Her concentration span is not long, and I'm afraid academic subjects do not interest her greatly."

Mum looked as if he'd slapped her face. "Miss Grant always gave her the most marvelous reports."

"She is indeed a delightful pupil. Her art — original. She is full of ideas. And in drama, her extrovert nature makes her . . . I am a great believer in drama work."

"But the scholarship?"

"As I say, if she works hard . . . would you like me to send home some work for her? Arithmetic, history, and geography — the examining body are very keen on these subjects."

"Oh, Mr. Edwards, would you? My husband and I are most anxious for Lily to have a proper education."

"I understand the senior school in Stroud is very good, Mrs. Freeman. And they ground girls thoroughly for careers."

Mum gave a good imitation of Dad's scornful look.

"Typing. Shop work. I know the sort of thing. I — we — want something better for Lily." She recalled her role and softened. "And like I told you, Mr. Edwards, I'd love Lily to go to my old school."

"Of course. We'll work toward that end. Won't we, Lily?" He included me in the indulgence. I blushed and stammered and held on to Phil's hand as if I were drowning. Which I was. Drowning in my own mortification. Because Mr. Edwards didn't think I'd get a scholarship like Ron.

Outside in the playground everyone milled around with their shaded flashlights, blowing steam into the night, stamping like horses. Dad was laughing somewhere with the Crakes and the evacuees refused to be rounded up into their various families and sang noisily, "We're going to hang out the washing . . ."

Phil tugged me over to the wall where even on this still, freezing night there was a breeze. There was an enormous view from the playground — Mr. Edwards said they'd chosen the most exposed spot to build the school to shrivel our bodies and expand our souls — and even in the darkness we were conscious of it spread out there below us.

Phil was at her most garbled. She yattered something in my ear, jumping up and down and nearly pulling my arm off.

"My help . . . my help you . . ." The words were strained through the cleft palate into nasal nonsense. A sudden wave of cold came up from the iced fields beneath; already my hands were dead.

Furiously I pulled off the knitted glove that matched my hateful pixie hood and snatched at my handkerchief to wipe Philippa's nose.

Aunt Florrie called above the hubbub, "Has Lily got Philippa? I hope they're not tearing around with those stupid Birmingham children. If Phil falls down —"

Outlined by flashlight came Freda, a very self-conscious medieval princess in her long satin gown. "Your mother's looking for you, Lil," she whispered, giggling. "I thought I'd die when you went up on the stage. You ought to be an actress, Lil — I thought I'd die —" The flashlight went out and she disappeared and the cold from below enveloped us again.

Philippa said, "My help you, Lil. My help you."

"What?" I looked at the outline of her and understood at last. The night was infinite and undemanding on one side of us, brief and noisy on the other.

"You'll help me with the scholarship," I repeated slowly.

She jumped again with excitement at my sudden realization and then she laughed. I had to laugh with her. It was funny after all. And then I hugged her. And we ran over to Aunt Florrie.

CHAPTER
THREE

Christmas came and went and still Dad was with us. I began to get bored with the war. It made hardly any difference to me except that Phil was with us and sometimes that was good and sometimes bad. It was good for Mum though. She forgot she was a foreigner and chattered away to Aunt Florrie and even Grandad.

And Phil did help me with my work in her way. She wouldn't let me go out even to do the firewatcher's plaques until I'd written something in my homework book, and she hung over my work admiringly so that I neatened up my writing and took great pride in underlining things in red ink. Mr. Edwards fingered his chin and said "Hmmm" a lot of times and darted me quick looks from his clear blue eyes and said I was taking more pride in my work. I trembled and prayed to God to help me get a scholarship so that Mr. Edwards would be pleased with me. I could recite all the countries in Europe to Phil, all the monarchs from William the Conqueror and I hardly ever got fathoms and furlongs mixed up.

When the first primroses were showing in the south-facing slopes, the vicar's wife came to see Mum.

"There's no question of you being compelled to take an evacuee, Mrs. Freeman." Her name was Mrs. Dorrit, but Mum and Aunt Florrie always called her Little Dorrit and went into fits of laughter. I didn't get it because she was a massive woman. "I do realize that your niece needs quiet, but with you and your sister at home all day that shouldn't be difficult. You see, Mrs. Freeman, we're at our wit's end. Some of the cottages — as you know — haven't even got indoor sanitation. And you have a bathroom."

Mum tucked a stray piece of hair back — a bad sign. Her hair only became ruffled when she was ruffled.

"I'll be honest with you, Mrs. Dorrit." That meant she was going to lie. "Philippa doesn't really get on with other children —"

"But I see her playing with Lily and her friends all the time. They were having a gay old time damming the stream only yesterday. Up to their knees in that icy water."

"*Philippa?*" Mum cast a horrified glance in the direction of the kitchen, where Aunt Florrie was trying a new recipe with grated cheese and egg powder. "Yes. Well. What I meant was — some children — strange children that is — are apt to be a little frightened of her."

"But they wouldn't be strange for long, would they?"

Mum poked the fire and hawed and hummed. She was in an awkward position. In spite of laughing at Little Dorrit she saw her as a possible ally. The Dorrits were even more foreign than Mum. And the vicarage was overflowing with the most ghastly of the evacuees.

"Perhaps just one. A girl." Mum temporized. "Younger than Lily. Nice and quiet."

Little Dorrit rose on the instant, her mission accomplished.

"You can choose your own, my dear. The train gets in tomorrow at three and they're coming up by bus from Gloucester. If you get to the village hall about four, you'll be in good time to pick what you want." It reminded me of the slaving days that Mr. Edwards was just telling us about.

Little Dorrit paused in the doorway, her natural-calf brogues planted far apart.

"Bring a box of Keatings with you," she instructed. "If you have a go straightaway, you might stop the lice getting in the house."

Mum tightened her mouth and almost slammed the door on her visitor before going to tell Florrie.

They huddled together at one end of the village hall and it was hard to imagine that in two or three days they would be running wild like the other evacuees. They were between five and twelve years old and they did not seem to be wearing proper clothes. The few topcoats were ripped and ill-fitting; most of them had knitted blankets wrapped around their shoulders and crossed in front, then pinned behind their waists. They smelled of horses and mice.

Mum didn't actually hold her nose as we went in but she tried not to breathe, which was the same thing. Mrs. Willis was there ahead of us looking frightened to death. She had held out against evacuees because the arranging was being done by Little Dorrit, wife of the Anglican vicar. But Mr. Edwards was fast bridging the gap between chapel and church and had persuaded her that we were all Christians, even the evacuees. She still didn't believe that and she approached the rabble much as a missionary approaches the cannibal's simmering stew-pot.

It made her turn even to Mum as to an old friend.

"Oh, Mrs. Freeman, isn't it awful? Just look at them."

Mum looked. "They can't help it," she said grudgingly. And then, "Thank goodness we've got a bathroom and a decent hot-water geyser."

Mrs. Willis took this the wrong way. "You can be just as clean with a hip bath in the scullery. Leastways normal people can."

I said quickly, "Where's Freda? Isn't she going to help you choose?"

"I wouldn't expose Freda to this!" Mrs. Willis was really shocked. "Mrs. Dorrit asked me to bring —" She opened her bag and gave us a quick glimpse of her flea powder. "So you can guess what they're like."

Mum said, "They'll get into the other children whatever you do. And I thought Lily ought to have a say in the matter as she'll be in the child's company more than anyone."

"What about . . . ?" Mrs. Willis raised her brows, heavily tactful. "Won't she be upset by a strange face in the household?"

I said rudely, "If you mean Philippa, no, she won't be upset. She likes people. Even the nasty ones."

Mrs. Willis started to look affronted and then laughed indulgently and said to Mum, "Lily's such a little firebrand. And the Freemans are all so placid."

Mum smiled right back. "She takes after me. She's very loyal." She put a hand on my shoulder. "Go and see if you can chum up with anyone, darling. The younger the better, remember."

I crossed the hall feeling protected by Mum's love. And I wondered if any of the evacuees had ever felt like I did. They were huddled in a corner as if there were a chalk line on the floor over which no one must step. The ones at the back were shoved against the wall, yet they made no attempt to push out a space for themselves. As I went I heard Mrs. Willis say, "There's no fear of Philippa's — er — complaint being catching, I hope?" And I understood in a blinding flash why Mum had never made any attempt to "get to know" our neighbors.

The girl was called Mavis Purton. We knew that because her blanket-shawl was labeled with her name and age; she was eight. She knew only one word, " 'Es." You had to ask her direct questions and if the answer was "No" she said nothing. We took her outside in the fresh spring air and unpinned her shawl. Beneath she wore the skimpiest cotton frock I had ever seen; her bare legs were red raw; her ankle socks were sodden wet and her shoes too tight and bursting out.

Mum shook the shawl, sprinkled Keatings over it, shook it again. Then she wrapped the girl up tightly and picked her up.

"Sod the fleas," she commented angrily as she carried her through the village. "God — to think we're fighting a war to keep this sort of thing going!"

Mum rarely swore.

I hopped up and down to look into the tiny monkey face.

"Tell me your name, then," I encouraged. "Come on, tell me what you're called." The brown eyes stared at me, then slid away. "Is it Mavis?" I asked, anxious to establish some kind of contact.

" 'Es," she whispered.

"See? She knows her name," I told Mum triumphantly. It was like fishing in Nanny Dexter's pond. After three hours of dredging with a net, even a tiddler can cause excitement.

Between us we got her home. She only weighed forty-two pounds, but that gets heavy after a bit so I gave her a piggyback when we'd passed the school. Her legs clung to me frantically, and her knickers were so wet it soaked right through my coat and sweater and vest and I stunk like she did. That was one thing about Phil, she very rarely wet her knickers.

Aunt Flo had taken Phil into Gloucester to see about elocution lessons, Dad was on late turn, and as soon as we came in the front door Grandad got up and went out the back saying somebody had better see to the hens before they all dropped dead. Considering they were his hens and were never fed before being penned for the night, this was unfair to say the least. We'd wanted to share Mavis with someone too; the strain was getting a bit much.

First of all Mum made her some cocoa.

"It's a good way of getting some milk into her straight off," she said to me, having given up addressing Mavis directly. "She's sure to like cocoa — probably been brought up on sweets and chocolate bars."

I smiled widely at the child. "D'you like chocolate?" I asked her cooingly.

" 'Es," she whispered.

She cried when all she got was cocoa, great welling tears without any sobs or hiccups. There was nothing we could do about it. We hadn't seen chocolate in the village shop since Christmas. In the end the tears stopped and she finished her cocoa and ate one of the little hard cakes Phil liked to make.

Then Mum took her up to the bathroom.

About fifteen minutes later there was a scream and I leapt up the stairs two at a time. Mum was standing in the bathroom staring into the bath. Everything was foggy from our grim, old gas geyser, but I could just make out Mavis' tiny emaciated figure squatting in the midst of the bath. Mum hurried out making choking noises in her throat. I peered closer through the mist. Two little turds bobbed over the surface of the water like small model boats. As I recognized them, Mavis gave a gigantic heave and threw up the cocoa and cake.

It was not a good beginning.

Strangely enough it was Grandad who coped with the bath.

Mum stood on the landing getting hold of herself, and he pounded up and took in the scene immediately.

"Get the kid out and wrap her up in a towel. Right out," he instructed me tersely. And he shut the door on me.

As Dad said later, "A great shit-shifter is my old dad," and he couldn't stop laughing as he said it.

Mum still didn't think it was funny. "The child's never seen a lavatory, let alone a bath," she repeated for the umpteenth time. "And her stomach can't take normal food."

"What's normal food?" Dad asked. "What's normal anything? Why should she have seen a bath or a lavatory?"

"You haven't got any standards, Albert Freeman," Mum said bitterly. "No wonder you don't think the war's worth fighting."

Dad's voice became very light and airy. "It was you who didn't want me to join up, Grace. Hey what?"

"Because we needed you here." She said "needed." Now that Aunt Florrie had come Mum was more self-sufficient. "But I wish . . . sometimes I wish . . ."

"What do you wish, Grace?" Dad asked casually.

She finished passionately. "I wish there was something you considered worth fighting for. Something you cared enough for —"

"Like King and country, hey what?" He caught me watching him and grinned. "Would you fight for King and country, Lil?"

I nodded fiercely and began to outline my plans for machine-gunning the Germans from the shelter of the sofa.

"Why would you do that, Lil?" Dad asked.

"Well . . . they'd shoot us if we didn't shoot them," I replied.

"What if they didn't? What if they didn't have guns? Just arrived and wanted to share the village? Like the evacuees."

I spluttered helplessly, "They're Jerries . . . dirty Jerries . . ."

"So you'd kill them because they're foreigners." He smiled at Mum. "But according to the village your mother and Aunt Florence are foreigners too, Lil."

It was very late. He had stopped on his way home for a quick one at the Plume of Feathers before they closed and I had come downstairs because I was hot and itchy. Mum bundled me out of the armchair and told me to take no notice of Dad; it was the beer talking.

I couldn't give up my idea of a Warsaw fight so easily, and I whined that I was hungry.

"What on earth's the matter with you, child?" Mum spotted me rubbing my leg and whipped up my night-dress. Flea bites notched my calf at regular intervals. She looked from Grandad to Dad. "This is the last straw," she said blankly. "Thank God Florrie and Philippa aren't here!" She dabbed with vinegar, and I yelped as it stung. "I could kill that Mavis!" she snapped.

"Let's kill everyone and be done with it, hey what?" Dad poked Grandad in the ribs and he guffawed. He'd been at the Plume of Feathers ever since the bath incident.

"They're drunk!" I crowed.

But Mum's face did not lighten.

CHAPTER
FOUR

It was Saturday the next day and I took Mavis out to play. We looked for primroses by Nanny Dexter's pond.

"D'you like flowers, Mavis?"

" 'Es."

"We get lots of flowers all over the hills in the summer. Violets next, then daffs, then cowslips, then bluebells and cuckoo flowers."

Silence.

She was wearing two of my old sweaters tied around the waist, my old Wellington boots, and socks, all miles too big for her. She just stood there looking at the grass.

"Which is your favorite flower?" I asked, forgetting.

No answer. Her eyes flicked like a little animal's, and she stared at the toe of her boot for a change.

"Bluebells?" I rephrased the question.

" 'Es."

I picked another primrose and made a small nosegay with some leaves and gave it to her. She held it woodenly.

"Or would you rather have primroses?"

" 'Es."

Some devil made me go on. "Daisies are your favorite though, aren't they?"

" 'Es."

"And you love frog spawn, don't you?"

" 'Es."

"Come on then. I'll find you some."

I dredged Nanny's pond with outstretched fingers and handed her a string of spawn. She held it. One hand of primroses, the other of frog spawn. It slithered and slipped and ran out of her tiny hand. and I shoveled it back into the pond impatiently. Mavis was no fun at all.

Ron and Freda came out of Nan's cottage and ran around the pond jumping and yelling. Freda? Jumping and yelling?

"Guess what — guess what —" Excitement made her laughter more asthmatic than usual. "Nan looked in the tea leaves for us and told us about the scholarship!"

Ron held his side. "Where's Philippa? Is this your evacuee? Wosser name?"

"Mavis. She only says yes. What did Nan say?"

"We're going to pass. Both of us. She saw it plain as plain —"

"Where's Philippa?" asked Ron.

"Gloucester." I turned to Freda. "It's only superstition. Doesn't mean anything."

"Oh, I know," Freda instantly agreed. But Ron looked surprised.

"She's nearly always right, is Nan. I don't want to go down to Gloucester every day to school. And all that homework, too. But Dad says I've got to."

His acceptance convinced me.

Freda said, "Hey, Lil. Why don't you ask her to tell your leaves? Go on. It's ever such a weight off your mind to know one way or the other. Go on, I'll come with you."

"I'm not supposed to go inside anywhere. Mavis has got nits in her hair, and Mum can't get them all out."

"So's ours." Freda loved to be the same as everyone else. One of the reasons she wanted to go to the high school was so she could wear the uniform. "Mum won't let her out of the house and everything is soaking in kerosene."

Ron said equably, "I get nits sometimes in my hair. Do yours itch, Mavis?"

"'Es." She almost smiled at him.

"We don't bother about 'm. My Gran d'say —"

Freda said, "Go on, Lil. Go and ask Nan about your scholarship. Unless you're scared, of course."

"She won't read the leaves for me. My mum had a word with her about it." I was glad. If I wasn't going to pass I didn't want Freda knowing about it this early in the year.

"She'll have to — being as how she's done ours. 'Twouldn't be fair else, and Nan's always fair."

"D'you want to go and see Nanny Dexter, Mavis?" Ron asked.

"'Es," breathed Mavis. I could have pushed her in the pond.

We sat around the ridged wooden table while Nan examined Mavis.

"Nothing wrong with 'er what the hills won't put right" was her verdict. "No one's took no notice of 'er before, so 'er'll be a long time talking and 'er needs food." For starters Nan fished in a jar and came out with a spoonful of gooey black currants from last year.

"She'll throw it up," I warned.

"Then we'll pack it down with a spud," Nan pulled out the ash box and clawed with her leathery, misshapen fingers. "Just salt to begin with. We'll work up to butter next time, cheese after that."

Mavis, who had ignored her boiled egg at breakfast time, wolfed the steaming potato silently and accepted another one.

"'Er's been brought up on sweets and chips, so that spud ain't going to upset her belly." Nan sat down and resumed work on her latest corn dolly. "Take no notice of her now. She'll pick things up as she d'go along." She looked up at me. "I suppose you want to know about that old scholarship now, do 'ee? Pour yourself a cup and drink it down, Lily-girl. I can't refuse you, and 'tis up to you whether you b'lieve the yarns I tell or no."

I looked at her, surprised. "I thought —" I began.

"I don't do it for a game, child. I told you that and I meant it. To help folks — put their minds at

39

ease . . . and there comes a time when I 'ave to do it, whether or no." She held my eyes. "Whatever folks d'say."

I swallowed. There was no getting out of it.

I poured my tea with bravado and swigged it down like Grandad knocking back a whisky. Then I passed her the cup. She swilled the dregs slowly and flicked the cup toward the fire. The flames hissed furiously and burned orange. She gazed into the cup.

There was a long silence except for Mavis' munching. Freda put her hand over her mouth to quench her whispered giggles. Ron stared solemnly at Nan in the same kind of trance as she was. The fire leaped with tall, pointed flames dancing toward the watery spring sunshine at the top of the chimney.

Nan spoke in a puzzled voice. "It says no . . . and then yes . . . I can't see proper. It's too close."

I stopped pretending I didn't care and pressed forward against her knee. "Which is clearer, Nan? The yes or the no?"

"'Tis too close," she repeated. "Time's pushing . . . two years . . . three mebbe. A fair man. And music." She stopped abruptly.

It was too like the gypsy fortune teller at the church fete who turned out to be Mrs. Mackless. I would have turned away except for that sudden halt.

"What, Nan? Can you see it now? What does it say?"

She put the cup into her lap. "'Tis all jumbled, Lily. I can't see anything after all."

"It was something nasty, Nan. Tell me. You've got to tell me." I held my breath. "Am I going to die, Nan?"

"Course not. Foolish child." Nan hugged me hard against her birdlike shoulder. "There was no death in your family that I could see. None at all —"

"What *was* it, Nan?" I wriggled free and stared at her beseechingly. "Was it that I wasn't going to get a scholarship?"

"I couldn't fathom out 'bout the scholarship at all. But in the far future . . . Well, don't make sense, Lily. You're not the sort to be alone. Must have been someone else stood there, all on their own."

"*Alone?*" I laughed with relief. "Is that all? Lonely? Honest — cross your heart? That's all it was?"

"That's all, Lily-girl. Cross my heart."

"And you don't know about the scholarship?"

Freda said, "You'd know if it had been yes, wouldn't you, Nan?"

Nan's voice sharpened. "And I'd have knowed if it had been no, too, my lady."

Ron was bored. "Let's go on with the dam. Dennis Crake will be down there already messin' it all about."

Mavis swallowed the last of her potato. "'Es," she whispered, cleaning her hands on my sweaters.

Nan came to the door and watched the others running off.

"You chose that little 'un because she was the runt, didn't you, my beauty?"

I shrugged. "I thought she wouldn't queen it over Philippa, that's all. Gosh — Phil can talk and she doesn't wet her knickers or mess in the bath."

Nan nodded. "True. But watch out for that little 'un, Lily. Watch out for her."

"Okay." I hesitated on the point of running. "Nan . . . it *is* all superstitious nonsense, isn't it, Nan? Like Mum says?"

Nan leaned down and put her toothless mouth to my cheek.

"Course 'tis, Lily. Why — this 'ere corn dolly I'm making now — I'm only doing it to stick pins in and kill someone off mighty quick. Now if that ain't daft, what is?"

I looked up, half startled.

"Who is it, Nan?"

She cackled horribly. "Mister 'Itler, Lily. Mister 'Itler 'imself!"

I laughed with her. The sun was stronger now and the slope beyond the pond invited a headlong run. The others were out of sight but I could hear Ron whipping up his imaginary horse like he always did. "Giddap — giddap there!" And Freda's stupid laugh was borne on the March breeze.

I left Nan and all her shadows and ran to join them.

That night Dad waited till we were all sitting around the table. Aunt Florrie was flushed with success. She had managed to get elocution lessons for Philippa, and Phil had enjoyed her first one and liked her "lady." Mum was smiling and tranquil after the furor with Mavis. Mavis herself ate two pieces of bread and marg and drank four cups of strong tea. Grandad grunted and pushed his bread larded with jam over to her.

Dad then announced that he'd joined up that day.

"The army," he said very lightly. "I'm being posted up to Yorkshire for training. The P.B.I., hey what?"

Mum went very still. Florrie threw her arms around him. Grandad muttered something about a "silly bugger" in a voice tight with pride.

"What's the P.B.I., Dad?" I asked.

"The poor bloody infantry. Just like I said, Lil. D'you remember?"

Mum smiled. "I thought after last night with Mavis it wouldn't be long before you went."

I took my turn at hugging him and was surprised to feel a little tremor right in the middle of his body.

"It's all right, Dad. You won't get killed. Nanny Dexter did the leaves today and she said no one in my family is going to die."

He hugged me to him but the tremor didn't stop, and Mum carried on alarming at me for going into Nan's with Mavis full of nits. I wished I hadn't told him.

We all went to the station to see him off and he had a travel warrant instead of his usual Great Western Railway privilege ticket.

He looked smaller and less significant than he usually did, and the porters and station foreman and even the stationmaster came up and shook his hand and wished him luck. The train snorted sulphurously in and he picked up his case.

"Well, Flo, you'll keep Grace company, I know that. And Dad, you'll keep an eye on all these women, won't you?" Grandad grunted and narrowed his eyes fiercely. "Lily. Don't worry about that scholarship, mind. Look where a high school education got your mother!"

Mum pressed her lips together, determined not to argue now.

Dad kissed Philippa, patted Mavis' shiningly clean brown hair, shook Grandad's hand up and down, up and down, knuckles white; then he caught Mum and me to him.

"I shall have a leave in six weeks, so don't let's get maudlin," he said.

"I'm not getting maudlin," Mum couldn't resist saying.

"What's maudlin?" I asked.

Dad kissed Mum on the mouth so hard I could see her neck muscles taking the strain.

"I might not know why I'm going, Grace. But at least I'm going," he said.

Sudden tears spurted out of my eyes. "I don't want you to go, Dad," I whimpered.

44

"Good God, girl. I shall be back before you know it. Stop crying — Lil, I've got to go now — stop crying —"

I hung on to him as he climbed into the train; I couldn't stop the tears.

He leaned out at an awkward angle. "Come on, Lil. Look — how about if Mum takes you to the shoe shop now for your new sandals? Eh? How about that? It's nearly summer and you could wear them home — break them in and get the feel of them —" I relaxed slightly. "Just let me go a minute, chookie, and I'll give you some money —" He only called me chookie when he was especially loving. I wept again and tightened my hold. The guard blew his whistle. Grandad and Mum tore my arms loose and slammed the door. Phil started her loud wailing.

Dad called, "Flo — take this pound for Lily — here you are!"

Aunt Florrie ran down the platform level with the train while Grandad and Mum held on to me, and Phil keened.

Mum said, "Lily — darling — show him a brave face. Give him a wave —"

I looked up and blinked. Mum was grimacing in the direction of the train's tail lamp and Grandad had his hand raised in a kind of salute. I wondered why we weren't supposed to let Dad see that we were miserable. But somehow I waved. Aunt Florrie returned and held Phil and she managed to wave too. The train rounded the bend, and we slumped and saw that Mavis was waving frantically and happily. Her legs beneath her new coat were soaking wet, and a pool widened on the platform between her feet.

I chose sandals with a diamond cutout again. Phil had red ones with pinpricks all over the fronts. Mavis couldn't try anything on because of her wet socks, but Mum promised she could have a pair the next time Phil went to Gloucester for her elocution lesson.

Grandad drove us home in our dear old GY 4396. I put my foot on the seat and traced the diamond with my finger. Phil reached over her long arm and held my toe in her hand. Between us Mavis was silently squashed. Dad had gone. Dad had gone. Was this what Nanny Dexter had meant by me being alone?

We went to the Shire Hall in a bus with Miss Jennings for the first part of the scholarship. Miss Jennings took the infants and couldn't control us. We ran up and down the aisle and straddled the seats, and she got flushed and prophesied doom for when we arrived. She was right. Our high spirits disappeared in the cathedrallike quiet of the lofty pillared hall. Adjudicators walked up and down and peered over our shoulders and into our laps. If we even went to the lavatory we were disqualified. The city children all wrote like mad and put up their hands for more paper and fresh ink. We wrote slowly with our tongues out. Audrey Mackless cried and was escorted outside by a lady with a mustache, and Dennis Crake just sat and stared gloomily at the frescoed ceiling.

Afterward Freda said hoarsely, "What did you put for the boy who had ninety-four bananas and gave four to his mother and seven to his father and shared the rest with his six brothers?"

"I said thirteen and five-sixths for each brother," I told her smugly.

"So did I." She breathed relief.

Ron said, "That's daft. How's he going to cut a banana up like that? I said he gave each brother thirteen and had five for himself." Trust Ron to be common-sensical.

Audrey Mackless gulped, "I couldn't read the question. It all jumped about in front of my eyes. I couldn't read it. Oh, I couldn't . . ."

Dennis Crake shouted, "Shut up, nit. It's better at Stroud Senior anyway. Only bloody snobs go to the high school."

Miss Jennings exploded at last.

"Dennis Crake! How dare you! Immediately we get back to school I shall tell Mr. Edwards that you have been completely out of hand the whole day! None of you deserve to get a scholarship!"

She did tell Mr. Edwards and he decided that we should take the infants into the playground and organize quiet games for them all afternoon. He and Miss Jennings sat in the shade of the horse chestnut tree marking books and chatting, and we sweated out all our frustrations in the sun with the pinnacled tower of Gloucester cathedral far beneath us in proper perspective.

CHAPTER
FIVE

At the end of May all the grown-ups were looking wide-eyed and sick. At home the wireless was always on and if anyone spoke during news time they were instantly shushed.

Grandad for once took the trouble to explain it properly.

"All us blokes what is left behind —" he managed to sound pathetic. "We're banding together to keep Hitler out and I got this map when we met at the village hall last night. Come on, Mavis — you listen too — you never know when you might be needed, my girl."

Philippa's eyes glazed over as they always did when Jerries or war was mentioned.

"Now when the Belgians packed it in last week, all our blokes got on the beach down here. See? Dunkirk? Jerry is sweeping over here, and down here — no, Lil, they went *around* the Maginot Line. So our boats went over — hundreds of 'em. Bloody hundreds. Nearly quarter million blokes they took off. That showed Hitler, eh? Didn't it show Hitler?"

"But we were beaten, Grandad," I pointed out. "He drove us off —"

"*Beaten?* What d'you mean, girl, beaten? How can we be bloody beaten when we've got our blokes safe back, laughing their heads off, all our men — experienced men, mind you — ready and waiting for him just to set one foot — one toe — on our country! And now we've got Winnie instead of that milksop Neville —"

"I liked Mr. Chamberlain," I objected, remembering the pantomime and the song we'd sung so cockily.

"Exactly!" He grunted mightily. "He was too bloody likeable, that was his trouble. What we need now is someone with a bit of fire in his belly —"

"News, Grandad!" called Aunt Florrie.

"Shush!" hissed Mum.

Mr. Churchill was speaking. I stood up and saluted solemnly, which always made Phil and Mavis splutter with suppressed giggles. But after a bit I sat down and we huddled together. Mr. Churchill made us feel like we felt when we were damming the stream and the dam kept breaking out in a new place and we had to feverishly pile up the stones and sods. When he said he could only offer us blood, tears and sweat, we shivered and shook but we didn't cry. Not even Phil cried.

When Mum came in to kiss me good night, I clung around her neck.

"Don't be scared, Lil." Her dark eyes were shining and brave. "We'll be all right."

"Oh I know." I wasn't a bit scared, only in an excited way. "It's just that I feel so old."

50

Mum gasped with laughter. "Old? Whatever makes you say that?"

"Well, first of all I wanted Dad to join up so that I could swank about him at school. Then I didn't want him to go at all and I was stupid and cried. Now . . . now I'm glad he's gone. Not because of the uniform or anything. Because it — it's glorious!"

She leaned back, considering the word.

"Reckon we're all getting a bit of the glory this time, Lily. There might be some fires for Florrie and me to look out for now."

My job of changing the plaques suddenly took on a new importance. I sighed and snuggled beneath the sheets. "I'm glad I was born when I was. I wouldn't want to miss the war."

Mr. Churchill had made heroes of us all.

Mr. Edwards came to see Mum; Grandad and I listened at the kitchen door.

"Your evacuee, Mrs. Freeman. Mavis Purton, isn't it? I'm afraid she's taking advantage of Lily's maternal instincts."

Grandad grunted in my ear and I had to agree with him. I didn't feel in the least maternal toward Mavis. She was a bore and a nuisance. I had to look on her as my war effort, otherwise she would have been unbearable. But Mum was agreeing with Mr. Edwards.

"I know she carries the child on her back to school. I've had a word with her about it — she could so easily do herself an injury. But I think she still does it."

We'd never get to school if I didn't.

"Miss Jennings is quite unable to communicate with her and if she's pressed too hard I'm afraid she urinates —"

Grandad and I looked at each other. You didn't have to press Mavis to get her to urinate.

"— and then nothing will console her until Lily is sent for."

I could imagine Mum's dark eyes snapping with annoyance.

"I know. It's just the same at home. Philippa or Lily . . . I'd think there was something wrong with the child mentally, only at times she can be so cunning."

"I agree with you entirely. Maybe when Lily leaves the village school Mavis will be forced to use some of that native cunning of hers to better purpose."

There was a pause. This was why I had been sent out of the room. I knew it quite suddenly and my heart jumped into my throat. If the news had been good I'd have been told. I knew before he spoke that I hadn't got through the first part of the scholarship.

He cleared his throat.

"I had a telephone call from the Shire Hall today. A friend of mine . . ."

Mum knew too. She sounded politely interested, as if any news from the Shire Hall was on a par with the weather.

"Really?"

"Yes. I thought I'd break the news unofficially before the post arrives tomorrow. Perhaps you can tell Lily. She's worked so hard over the past six months. I do hope she won't be terribly disappointed."

Mum said, "Her father went to Stroud. I think that will help."

Mr. Edwards coughed again. "The standard is very high and there are only six places for girls from the whole of the country. We're very lucky to get one of them."

Another short pause, just long enough for Mum to swallow.

"Freda Willis?" she asked.

"Yes. Freda's got a brain like a sponge. Whether she will be able to use the facts she soaks up — that is another thing." I could hear him sigh through the thick door. "I've watched Lily this last half year, Mrs. Freeman — she hasn't so many facts as Freda has, but she could have used them to good effect."

Mum said as if comforting him, "Never mind. If there's good in her it will come out wherever she goes to school and whatever happens."

I was hanging on to the door knob, my hand taking the weight of my heavy body. I remembered Mrs. Crake describing a funeral she'd attended and the chief mourner — "bowed down with grief." I'd laughed at the time but now I knew it was possible. I couldn't have got myself upright without Grandad's help. He held me against his chest, quite still and silent so that they wouldn't hear us in the living room.

Mr. Edwards rallied. "Of course you're right. But I'm very sorry indeed. At least Ron is through. I think I'd have taken a gun and shot them down at the Shire Hall if he hadn't."

Mum managed to laugh. "When do they go down again for the oral?"

"Two or three weeks I believe. It's practically a formality . . ."

Grandad half carried me to the back door. The sun was still hot although it was evening. We weren't far past the longest day in the year. I took great gulps of air and then I stood up by myself.

Grandad whispered in my ear, "Go on, chookie. Fly free for a while and get used to it." He shoved me gently outside. "Go on. It still belongs to you just as it was before."

I ran straight as an arrow up the track, across the road and down the long slope to Nan's. The fields and hedgerows descended in great leaps to the plain around the Severn River, all a muted green-blue in the light. Too exposed. I slithered down a bank and forced my way through brambles and came to the stream. It was bordered by willows and there was one special one near our dam with a branch low enough to straddle and shin along . . .

Willows are peculiar trees. Their trunks end quite suddenly in a shallow cup, and their branches all sprout whippily from the edge of the cup. Inside those branches I was like a bird in a nest. The floor was dry and powdery with old wood, and I pushed myself into it much as a bird does in a dust bath. I wanted to become part of the tree and grow with it. That was all a tree had to do to be successful. Just grow and be there.

I hadn't failed in anything before. I could slide on ice, climb trees, ford streams as well as any boy three or four years my senior. I could run faster than all the girls and half the boys in my class. I was an only child with no competition at home — I knew I came first with Mum even before Dad. That probably I came first with Dad, too, though I wasn't so certain of that. Even silent, grunting Grandad boasted of my prowess down at the Plume of Feathers . . . until now.

I gazed through my screen of willow wands at the four spires of the cathedral and tried to face the fact. A whole wedge of my heritage was suddenly gone. I would never slide those high school banisters sidesaddle from form room to form room like Mum had. Never take part in the special carol service, holding my candle, part of a crocodile of candles, winding throughout the school until the whole building was filled with soprano voices. I would never queue at the sweetshop and wait about on the muddy hockey field and watch the annual outdoor performance of *A Midsummer Night's Dream* and battle with the intricacies of a foreign language and . . .

I forced myself to stop remembering Mum's reminiscences and consider the immediate future.

Freda. I squeezed my eyes shut and screamed inside my head. Mr. Edwards . . . I had disappointed him. And Mum. Mum would suffer for me. Mum's staunch loyalty and cheerfulness would be harder to bear than Freda's whispered condolences.

At last I swung out of my nest, almost deliberately skinning my knee on the way down. By the time I reached Nan's cottage door the blood had run down into my sandal. Nan thought it was the reason for my visit.

"Now just sit you here while I wring out a rag." There was no running water in the house but the well was only just outside and Nan kept a pail brimful for drinking. She plunged a strip of rag into this and sponged at my leg. " 'Tisn't like you to scrawp yourself raw, my girl." She looked up. "You a bit tarny about something?"

Confronted by her walnut of a face, I lost my pride and I wept.

"I haven't got the first part of the scholarship, Nan. I'm not going to Mum's school."

"A-a-a-h." She pressed the makeshift dressing hard on my leg and I gasped. "So. The leaves were wrong."

I had to be honest. "They said yes and no . . . Oh, Nan, I wanted to go and I've worked hard and Phil's helped me —" Philippa. She would be empty-eyed about this. Probably she would start rocking herself.

Nan pressed harder still and I stopped crying to protest. The bleeding had stopped.

56

"'Tedn't right that. 'Tedn't right at all, Lily. They shouldn't say yes if they mean no." She sat back in her chair, frowning.

"Well, you did warn me it was all superstition." I was the comforter and began to feel better. "You said —"

She snapped, "I know what I said, my girl. And I know what's real and what's superstition. The leaves were wrong and that's that."

She made me feel faintly guilty for making the leaves wrong. I asked for a potato. She jabbed her finger at the grate and I fetched two, cut them carefully, sprinkled salt, and handed her one. We munched dourly.

Then she said, "Fetch me old 'Itler, Lily. He's in that there biscuit tin next to the jar of last year's plums."

I fetched the tin. The corn dolly was rough compared with her usual marvelous spirals and convolutions. The straw was ragged and and chopped off at the top — I suppose to represent Hitler's cowlick.

She fished in her hat and produced a long hat pin.

"Here," she said, handing it over. "Give him a few bloody good jabs. You'll feel better."

We sat there, eating potato, the light growing orange as the sun went down behind Gloucester's smoke. And we speared the corn dolly until it lay in shreds on the ridged wooden table.

Then I went home.

CHAPTER
SIX

Mum said, "I'm not sorry, darling. Gloucester is a long trip every day and with the possibility of air raids . . . I wouldn't have a minute's peace."

Aunt Flo said, "At least you haven't got to wear that awful uniform, Lily. They might ration clothes later on and imagine having to use all your allowance on that!" Aunt Flo had never been to the high school.

Phil wailed and Mavis smiled slightly and after Mr. Edwards had made his announcement during prayers, Freda came up to me in the playground and said, "I'm real mad you didn't get it, Lily — I don't know how I'm going to go down to Gloucester all by myself each day."

Mavis wet herself twice in the morning and once in the afternoon but Mr. Edwards wouldn't let me go through to the infants' room. She was drowning in her own tears when she met me by the horse chestnut tree to go home.

"I'm not allowed to carry you either, Mavis," I told her sternly. "Mr. Edwards says I'm spoiling you. You'll never bother to use the lavs if I keep coming in and changing your knickers. And you won't be able to run in the sports if I keep carrying you. And if I do your work for you you'll never learn to read."

She walked beside me sniveling. Gradually a resolve hardened inside me and when we got out of the village I sat down on the slippery grass at the side of the road.

"You're going to learn your letters, Mavis," I said sternly. "I'll make Mr. Edwards proud of me somehow. I'm going to teach you to read."

"'Es," she hiccuped.

I traced the alphabet in the dust. It took ages and there was a little breeze that blew it away now and then. It took up about twelve yards of road. I marched her along telling her the sounds each letter made. Then we went back to the beginning.

"Now you're going to do it. There's no one to hear you talk and the letters are big enough . . ." She was staring at her feet and I yanked her head up. "You're going to do it, Mavis."

"'Es," she whispered.

"Right. Start. NOW!"

She just went on standing. I shook her quite hard.

"Go on! Do it — start!"

She began to snivel again and looked right and left along the road. It was completely deserted. Her sniveling reached whimper proportions.

"Mavis, I know you can do it. If you don't start telling me the sounds of those letters I'm going to hit you."

She stopped crying long enough to slide her eyes up to mine and away and she grinned to herself.

I stepped back and whacked her across her soggy bottom. She yelped, but I hadn't hurt her so she went on crying quietly. I did it again. Her mouth tightened. I did it again.

"Stroller!" she whispered spitefully.

It was the local term for children who went to Stroud Senior School. For all her silent weeping, she had picked it up and knew what it meant. She also knew that on that particular day it was an insult.

I stared at her for a moment while it soaked in. She stared back, not a bit frightened because she knew I'd never really hit her. A sly little smile was in her eyes.

I swung at her face with all my might. She was still tiny and fragile and she went with the blow and fell like thistledown on the grass. I stared at the crumpled figure in icy horror.

Then she got up, cringing, terrified at last, a bare elbow held protectingly over her head. She didn't look at me. Just went to the beginning of the long line of letters.

"Ah . . . Bu . . . Ku . . . Du . . ." she went down the line phonetically, hiccuping, shuffling, rubbing at her snotty nose until her whole face was covered in slimy mud. She knew all the letters.

She wouldn't meet my eyes afterward, and I didn't know what to say to her anymore.

At last I squatted down and waited and eventually she came over and climbed onto my back and we jogged home.

After that she would speak to Phil and me, and we would transmit her messages to the grown-ups. But in other ways she was more of a burden than ever. Or maybe it was my guilt. But at least I'd discovered Dad was right in one thing. I'd never be able to kill the Jerries if ever they came down our track.

Dad came home on leave.

It was three months since we'd seen him, and at first we put down the change to his haircut and uniform and loss of weight. But it was more than that. He wouldn't tell us about his training, dismissed the war as "the usual cock-up," and hoped that Mr. Churchill was going to put his money where his mouth was.

"Look how he organized Dunkirk," Mum reminded him, unable once again to resist an argument.

"Have you seen anyone from the Expeditionaries?" Dad asked. "No? Well, some of them came to our camp afterward. They could tell you a thing or two about how well it was organized."

Grandad said, "Hang about, lad. Quarter of a million blokes we shifted from those bleeding beaches —"

"Exactly. We shifted. The people of this country who owned boats. They went out and shifted them."

"Six destroyers were lost —"

Dad looked around with an expression we'd never seen before. It silenced us. He said, "I'll tell you this, then I don't want to talk about it anymore. If I'd known what a shambles it was, I'd never have gone. I'd have stuck to my reserved job like a limpet even if the whole village had said I was a coward and sent me white feathers." He stood up. "I'm going to bed. I hope to sleep for twenty-four hours."

Grandad, who had hoped for a drinking companion that night, snorted loyally at the closed door. "He needs some action. And he knows he won't get any now we're under siege."

"Under siege." More words for my private collection. Stoical words that did not lack courage but had nothing to do with actually shooting anyone.

Dad's leave might have been a catastrophe, but on the third day something completely out of the blue happened.

We were in the living room eating our tea around the table. Philippa had been to Gloucester for her elocution and something had upset her; she sat looking at her strawberries — we had a bumper crop that year — and rocking unhappily. Grandad got stuck into his dish with grunts of annoyance; he hated it when Philippa displayed what Mum and Aunt Flo called her "symptoms." Mavis had finished her fruit and was wiping the sugary syrup with her bread and butter and eyeing Phil's dish, when there was a knock at the door.

Aunt Florrie said, "It can't be Little Dorrit. She goes to the front."

Dad half rose. "Let me get out. I don't want to be here for one of your interminable yawping sessions."

Mum said soothingly, "It'll be someone for Lily. Freda Willis, I expect."

And then the door opened and there was this wide-shouldered figure in the sort of suit you didn't see anymore — light-gray pinstripe double-breasted with big revers, topped by a black homburg on Viking-fair hair.

Aunt Florrie did her Joan Crawford to perfection. She stood up, gripped the edge of the table, and made a moaning sound in her throat. Phil just went on rocking. Mum, Dad, and Grandad stared. It was left to me to scream at the top of my voice: "Uncle Bert!"

It was indeed Uncle Bert. The fact that he had been inexplicably missing for nearly a year didn't seem to bother him in the least. He came forward, his wonderful smile wide, carefree, all-embracing. I flung myself on him and he lifted me against his suit, strawberry-sticky fingers and all, and I put my face on his smooth neck and smelled again the freshly-bathed smell of him and knew so well why Aunt Florrie had left behind her nice steady boyfriend in Gloucester and gone off with the handsome stranger that day on Southend Pier.

Dad wasn't far behind me with his welcome. Although he had sniped at Uncle Bert in his absence, whenever he appeared in the flesh Dad got on well with him. Everyone did. No one could stand against his charm. Dad clapped him on the shoulder and said something about the bad penny. By which time Aunt Flo was in tears and Phil was wailing. Uncle Bert put me down and opened his arms wide to gather them to him. His laughter seemed to absorb their anguish, dry it up like the sun.

"Blimey me ole china," he said to Aunt Florrie in a funny Cockney twang. "What a welcome. But you're as beautiful as ever. My God, but you're beautiful." She looked up at him, her dark eyes swimming. There were no reproaches. He clasped Phil just long enough and then lifted Aunt Flo off the floor. "How have I lived without my lovely women?"

Phil smiled and held the edge of his jacket.

Grandad grunted and said he'd got to feed his fowls if no one else had anything to do. Uncle Bert stopped him and dragged in an enormous suitcase. It was entirely packed with whisky and gin bottles. Grandad's eyes lit up. I glanced back at the table. Phil's strawberries had all disappeared and Mavis was licking her lips.

We all went to Symonds Yat for a picnic. All except Grandad, who thought the idea was crazy; in any case we couldn't have got anyone or anything else inside GY. Mavis sat on Uncle Bert's knee in the front next to Dad; Mum, Aunt Florrie, Phil, and me wedged somehow into the back. Aunt Florrie had made Phil and me matching frocks out of an old dance dress of hers. They were rose colored with big penny-sized white spots all over them. We had white cotton socks beneath our sandals and Uncle Bert had given us hair slides with enamel butterflies on them. We were in heaven.

We drove with the windows down and Dad switched off the engine going down the hills to save petrol, and the summer air, heavy with gorse, filled the car. We had to shout to hear each other.

Mum said, "We missed the salt, Florrie — those hard-boiled eggs will be nothing without salt. Lily, you'll pick a hole in that new frock if you don't stop smoothing it like that."

Aunt Florrie leaned across and put my hand on Phil's knee, then Phil's hand on top of mine, then my other hand, then Phil's.

"A hand sandwich," she called out. "Look, Phil, a hand sandwich."

Phil laughed and jumped up and down, causing GY to career from one side of the road to the other.

"Saaam . . . widge," she repeated, delighted. "Saam-widge."

"For Pete's sake keep still!" Dad shouted.

"There. Did you hear that, Bert? She's getting on well with her lessons, isn't she?"

I held Phil down, stifling my giggles against her bare arm.

Mum yelled, "Florrie — the salt —"

Uncle Bert suddenly struck up the National Anthem, his hand across his eyes in a mock salute.

"I can't bring myself to die for my country," he announced sonorously. "But I will make the next best supreme sacrifice. I will eat hand sandwiches without salt!"

The car zigzagged again as we all rocked with laughter, even Dad. As soon as that bout was over, Uncle Bert lifted Mavis to the roof and examined his pale-gray trousers.

"Christ." He looked around at us lugubriously. "You didn't tell me this was a leaky model!"

We parked right on the edge of the Wye and we all went swimming in the crystal clear water. Mavis didn't want to, but Mum made her. She sponged Uncle Bert's trousers too and laid them out on the sheep-bitten grass. Uncle Bert dried off in his swimming costume and then put on his socks and shoes to show us how Herr Goering dressed over in Berlin.

"They're all bonkers," he declared knowingly. "They go to bed in their boots so that if they have to get up for a pee they can click their heels."

Dad lay on his back, his hands behind his head, more relaxed than he'd been since he had come home.

"Good job we've got you around to show us how it's done," he commented lazily in between our shrieks of incredulous laughter. "If they get over here you'll be invaluable, Bert."

"You can mock!" Uncle Bert pointed a reproachful finger. "But you'll have cause to be grateful to me when I save you all from the firing squad." He strutted up and down in front of the spread tablecloth on which Mum was laying the picnic. "I shall go to meet them dressed like this — maybe minus the costume. I shall salute —" He shot his arm up in the Hitler salute. "I shall tell them I've always been a secret Nazi — they'll make me Gauleiter of Gloucester —"

We rolled about in convulsions.

On the other side of the river another picnic party stared across the water in consternation. Uncle Bert walked toward them until he was ankle deep in water — shoes, socks, and all.

"*Heil* Hitler!" he yelled. "The glorious German army have landed at Dover! *Heil* Hitler!"

The picnickers watched as Aunt Florrie tried in vain to restrain him. Then, no doubt thinking we were an outing from a lunatic asylum, they got into their car and drove hurriedly away.

"You're awful, Bert," Aunt Florrie said, flushed and half annoyed. "They might report us or anything."

He grinned at her menacingly. "All English women must be ground under the heel of our German heroes!" He scooped up a handful of water and advanced on her. "Come here, my English blackbird! Sing for your supper!"

She screamed. "Bert! Stop it this minute — d'you hear me?"

He chased her down the shore, completely ridiculous in his soggy shoes and socks. At intervals he shouted "*Heil* Hitler!" at the top of his voice.

Mum suddenly threw off her sandals and ran into the water and splashed it back at Dad. He rolled over and eyed her and she did it again. Slowly he got to his feet. "Right . . ." he said. "Righto . . ."

We ate our picnic half an hour later. We were all absolutely soaked to the skin. My new frock was plastered to me. We were happy.

When we got back home there was a message from Grandad that he was waiting at the Plume of Feathers, and Mum and me had to go and see Mr. Edwards. Uncle Bert and Dad wasted no time in piling back into GY and driving off. Mum packed Mavis up in an old towel and rubber knickers and put her to bed, then she and I walked slowly into the village to the schoolhouse. Mum said if there were any more complaints about Mavis she would insist on her being sent to a special school, but she didn't mean it. Somehow the worse Mavis got the more we were saddled with her.

It was a golden evening, and my dress had dried out without the dire shrinking Mum had prophesied. My hair — unfortunately just missing Mum's raven black — had dried fluffily and with my enamel slide I was convinced I looked like Deanna Durbin. I smiled hard with my mouth closed, which forced a couple of dimples into my cheeks, and waved happily to everyone we saw. There weren't many people around luckily. On Sunday evenings you were either at church, chapel, or the Plume of Feathers.

The schoolhouse was small and gray, its tiny windows buried in the chunky Cotswold stone, the front door smothered in a rambler rose. Mr. Edwards — who should most certainly have been at chapel with the Willises — was gardening. He looked unfamiliar with his shirt sleeves rolled to his elbows and his suspenders showing.

"Mrs. Freeman." He straightened, his hand in his back like Grandad. He was lifting potatoes. "And Lily. Your grandfather told me you would be back from your picnic around this time." He had missed chapel for us. Missed Freda.

He held up a potato bearing a "head" complete with eyes and nose. "What does this remind you of?"

"Goering." I giggled remembering Uncle Bert in his shoes and swimming costume.

Mr. Edwards looked again and nodded. "Not unlike. Not unlike at all." His clipped Welsh accent made it matter-of-fact and unfunny. He laughed rarely.

We went inside the house. It was much smaller than ours but very neat and cozy. A fire was laid in the hearth and there was no smattering of ash on the gleaming tiles.

"Sit down. Sit down both of you. That's the way." He straddled a chair opposite us. "As you know the oral examination for the high schools takes place on Monday morning. Well . . ." He couldn't repress his own excitement. ". . . My friend from the Shire Hall telephoned me this morning to tell me that one of the candidates — a girl — has withdrawn, as she is moving from the city." He paused again and drew a deep breath. "That leaves a free place which may be filled by the girl who gained the next best marks in the written exam. That girl is you, Lily."

Mum and I sat there very still staring at him. Then we looked at each other.

"Lil. You've done it," Mum breathed.

Mr. Edwards was beaming openly. He was proud of me. Mum was proud of me. And Nan's leaves hadn't been wrong at all. So it followed that if they'd been so accurate about the scholarship, they would be accurate about other things. None of us would die.

CHAPTER
SEVEN

The high school was big.

That was my only impression for at least a month. Freda got the hang of its geography within the first few days, and without her I'd have been completely lost because we changed rooms for each lesson and it never occurred to me that Room 26 was probably on the top floor whereas Room 4 was likely to be on the ground.

She also kept me abreast of things academically. My bewilderment and gradually descending misery were so great that I honestly could not understand what the teachers said. With difficulty I grasped that they weren't even called teachers. They were mistresses. Perhaps that was why they were so impossible to understand.

Uncle Bert took us down and brought us home in GY most days. He had a job in the aircraft factory now and if he had to work overtime he stayed in Gloucester overnight. Then Mr. Willis used some of the petrol allocated to the farm and ferried us back and forth. We had to hang about until six o'clock for Uncle Bert in any case. Sometimes we window-shopped; sometimes we'd go into Fearis' and treat ourselves to tea and toasted tea cakes; sometimes we'd explore the docks and look at the prison or walk down St. John's Lane into the gaslit secondhand shops. Because of Mum, I knew Gloucester well and would have been the ringleader in these forays normally. But nothing was normal anymore.

One dim October afternoon we were hanging about in the cathedral. Freda was in the cloisters doing her homework, and I sat numbly listening to Ron and watching the colored patterns made by the east window. I was somehow unable to do my homework with Freda, unable to assemble my recollections of the day into any kind of pattern.

Ron broke off suddenly and looked at me.

"Anything wrong, Lil?" he asked.

"Nope."

"You keep starin' and starin' at that window . . . Hey, did you know they've taken the west one out and wrapped it all up and put it down in the crypt? The crypt here, that is. Not my bloody school. Though come to think of it, that's a bit like a musty ole cellar, too." He laughed and waited for me to join in. When I didn't, he fell silent again.

"Hey, Lil," he said at last. "You sure nothing's wrong?"

"Sure."

"You hate it at the high school and you don't want anyone to know. That's it, isn't it?"

I managed to tear my gaze away from the window.

"How did *you* know? You're a bit too sharp for your own good, Ron Morgan."

He grinned, then stopped grinning. "Tell the truth, Lil, you looked a bit like Mavis looks sometimes. Kind of . . . blank."

A few short weeks ago that would have been an insult. Now it was quite simply the truth. This was how Mavis felt. No patterns. No sense. Nothing. I tried to laugh it off.

"At least I don't wet my knickers."

He tried to laugh too, but the fact that I hadn't denied it vehemently struck home. He fidgeted uncomfortably.

"Have you told your mum how you feel?"

"Nope."

"You tell your mum everything. You always have."

"Not this time. She wanted me to go to her old school. She thinks it's heaven."

"Tell Philippa then. She'll understand."

I could have hit him. "Don't be daft. Phil's never been inside the village school let alone the high school. She wouldn't know what I was talking about."

"But she'd understand. That it was foreign and unnatural to you." He changed the subject abruptly. "Why don't you come and help with the dam at weekends? Audrey Mackless said you were getting stuck-up because of the scholarship."

Unexpected tears were blocking my nose.

"I can't. It's as if everything that matters — everyone that matters — is behind a curtain or something. It's just getting up early and living through the day till four. Telling Mum it was fine. Doing my homework somehow. Trying to get to sleep early so that I can get up early ... it's terrible."

In the face of my distress he stopped being embarrassed.

"Poor old Lil. I didn't know it was like that. I hate it — of course. I knew I should. But as soon as I'm away from it, it's gone —"

"In any case, it can't *get* at you —" I wanted to explain now, I wanted to talk. "You're a whole person . . . I don't know. You're sure of yourself. You belong to the hills and they belong to you. I thought they belonged to me, too, but they're not protecting me. Perhaps it's something to do with me being a hybrid." I looked at him despairingly. "It's as if I've got no clothes on, Ron —" I plucked at my navy gaberdine, the school uniform raincoat. "I'm standing there in that awful huge place and there's a wind blowing right through to my soul."

He put his face right in front of me. Why had I never seen before how beautiful he was? His bumpy country nose, big horse teeth, clear gray — almost colorless — eyes.

All he said was, "It'll be all right, Lil. It'll be all right."

It was such a relief to have told him that I pressed myself back in my pew and tried to get hold of myself. And after a bit he began to talk about something else. At least I thought it was something else.

"Phil *knows* what's right. She just knows it. She works with things, not against them. Summer, winter — she knows there's a time for everything." He became animated. "You know how she hates talking about the war?" I managed a nod. "Well, last Sunday — you weren't there — we found a dead rabbit and I thought, Hey-up, we're going to have a wailing session now. But she looked at it and didn't make a sound. It was natural. See?" I nodded again. I didn't see but I wanted him to keep talking.

He went on eagerly, "She feels things, does Phil. She can't think them out like we can and she can't talk about them. But she feels them all the same."

I wanted very much to hold his hand. "You're like that, Ron. You . . . you're in harmony."

"What?" He looked startled as if I'd changed the subject. Then he laughed out loud and a scurrying verger looked disapprovingly along our pew. "No, Lil. You got me wrong." He frowned. He wasn't in the habit of thinking about himself. "I just . . . live. I do what I've got to do . . . school and peeling the spuds for Gran and helping Grandad to dress. Then I do what I want to do."

Freda appeared in the door of the cloisters and I could have killed her. We wandered outside and along Westgate Street to the Cross, and I wondered whether I could break a leg or get chicken pox, which was the only child's ailment I hadn't had. If only . . . if *only* the high school could get bombed.

We waited till half past six and Uncle Bert hadn't come. I began to live out my current nightmare that I couldn't get home at all. It was a gray windy evening, the light nearly gone. Freda grumbled incessantly, Ron was silent.

We started walking.

Freda said, "Audrey Mackless' mum went to a Spitfire whist tournament down at the aircraft canteen. She saw your Uncle Bert there."

"Not surprising. He works there," I said wearily.

"He was with someone else."

"He's never on his own. Not Uncle Bert."

"Another woman," Freda said with relish.

I didn't flare up as I would have done last summer.

"He's very popular. He can't help it —"

"He didn't try very hard, so Mrs. Mackless said."

All sorts of small things flitted through my mind. Aunt Flo's thinness and the rows that sometimes sprang up at weekends.

"If you're hinting at anything, Freda Willis, just shut your mouth. He brings us home most nights so he doesn't get much chance to meet other women, does he?"

"Like tonight?" she said, sweetly sarcastic. "And anyway, when he stops the night in Gloucester Mrs. Mackless says he isn't working overtime at all. Mrs. Mackless says —"

Ron snapped, "Shut up, Freda! Here's a car . . . no, not yours, Lil, but a car."

They were few and far between, and this was one of the first to be equipped with a floppy, floating gas bag on the roof. Even I had spotted it in the staff car park at school.

Freda said, "It's Miss Crail!" She waved excitedly. I discovered later that Miss Crail was a Latin mistress so we didn't even have her. Trust Freda to recognize her.

She drew up with a yelp of brakes. Freda spoke to her breathily, Ron politely with his cap held in his hand. It turned out she had a cottage at Haresfield not two miles below our village and had had the gas bag fitted so that she could get home every evening.

"Do let me give you a lift," she said. She was pretty, with dark-red hair and eyes to match. "Your uncle will realize what has happened and come on home, won't he? Jump in."

We jumped in, Freda in the front, Ron and me behind. There was polite conversation. Miss Crail thought it well worth living so far from her work. She loved getting out of the river mist and high up in her "little eagle's nest." Freda agreed fervently and with a lot of gasps.

"We've lived in the hills since Grandad can remember," Ron said, coming out of his shell suddenly. "We d'know a lot of the Haresfield folk."

"You wouldn't know me." Miss Crail laughed at him in the mirror. She had a crooked tooth that sort of caught on her underlip. "I bought the cottage when I got my post at the high school a year ago. I'm from Yorkshire."

"Oh." Ron sat back again. "A foreigner."

"Yes," she agreed. "A foreigner indeed." She laughed at him again in the mirror and sheepishly, unwillingly, he smiled back.

Uncle Bert never turned up that night and Aunt Florrie didn't ring up the factory or anything. Miss Crail took us each to our own doors and told Mum that any time we wanted a lift she would be only too pleased. Mum was delighted with her. So was Ron. Whether Uncle Bert came or not, he waited for Miss Crail. Freda waited with him. Then Uncle Bert stayed in Gloucester all week because there was no petrol for GY. I went to school with Miss Crail too. And somehow I couldn't talk to Ron anymore so I took his advice and told Philippa about my new life. Sometimes I went on talking until far into the night and she put her long arms around me and rocked me with her until I fell asleep.

Aunt Florrie was white-faced as she told us her plans.

"I didn't want to go behind your backs . . . we're so happy here with you. But my duty — my first duty — is to Bert. And — and — it's so quiet up here in the hills. He needs — he has to have — company. Try to understand, my dears. Grace — you know how it is." Mum kept looking at her breakfast plate. Mrs. Mackless had been talking in the village shop when Mum went for the rations. Mrs. Mackless talked everywhere.

Aunt Flo put her arm around Philippa.

"Last time I left Phil for her elocution lesson I went to the house agents. There were a lot of houses to let — people don't want to live in the city with all the bombers going over. D'you remember Lake Road, Grace? The lake's a static water tank now but the cottage is still there. There's room for visitors ... and" — her voice shook — "and Bert says he will settle down there if I make a home —"

Grandad said incredulously, "You're not leaving? You know how Grace is fixed out here —" He caught Mum's eye and grunted. "Well, and what about the child? She's at home up here, thanks to Lil. Everyone accepts her."

Phil didn't understand. She moved her head from one speaker to the other and smiled gently. Surprisingly, Mavis started dribbling tears onto her toast. I felt nothing. Nothing at all. I grasped that Aunt Florrie and Phil were leaving after over a year and that Mum would miss them very much. That night Phil started wailing and I heard Aunt Flo go in and try to comfort her. I could have gone too — as she had done for me — but I didn't. I stared blindly into the darkness and thought of school the next day.

Miss Crail took us home as usual with Ron all starry-eyed and Freda giggling and me silent. It was dark when she dropped me off at the top of the track. I was the last one.

She said, "Are you all right, Lily?"

"Yes."

"I think you might have flu coming on. Why don't you have the day in bed tomorrow?"

"I'm all right."

I walked down the track. It was raining that gray, relentless November rain, but I didn't feel it. I went in the back door and Mum was cooking my favorite tea, toasted bacon sandwiches. No one else was around.

"Where's Mavis?" I asked, thinking it was Phil's day for elocution — I'd lost all count of the days.

Mum jerked her head. "By the fire. Grandad's reading to her."

"*Grandad?* Reading to Mavis? What's up?"

Mum met my eyes. Hers were coal black. "They've gone, Lil. Aunt Flo thought it would be better if she slipped off while you were both at school. Mavis is very upset."

I looked back at her without emotion.

"They've only gone to Gloucester. I go there every day and no one gets upset about that."

A flicker of surprise twitched Mum's face. "Well . . . Mavis won't see much of Phil now. They were close."

"Were they?" Jealously stabbed me; a new physical pain.

I walked woodenly into the living room. Mavis was sitting on the floor — Grandad would never have her on his lap because of her habits — and he was coming to the end of the story. He read without any expression at all but she gazed at him, entranced. I waited until he finished.

"Did Phil use to sit with you when you had bad dreams, Mavis?" I asked tersely.

Mavis' eyes spilled over with tears; Mum tutted at me while Grandad grunted.

" 'Es," whispered Mavis.

A vestige of pride stirred somewhere in me.

"You can come in to me if you're scared," I managed to bring out before going upstairs to change out of my loathsome uniform.

That night for the first time in months the siren wailed and Grandad marshaled us on the landing with a gleam of enthusiasm in his eye. He had dug an air-raid shelter at the beginning of the summer and all he'd done for the last month was bail it out after each storm.

"Slippers. Blankets. Candles. Gas masks," he recited briskly.

Mum said wearily, "It'll be nothing, Dad. Let's stay in bed — the girls need their rest."

"Don't be ridiculous, Grace. You can hear them above the guns."

We could too. The typical pulsating drone of the German air armada once again. We stumbled down the stairs, tripping over our blankets. It was still pouring down outside and Mum tried to hold an umbrella over Mavis and me as we ran past the chicken coop.

"Don't waste time," Grandad ordered. "Use your flashlight, Lily — shade it, girl, shade it. Don't light any candles, we don't want to give ourselves away."

We fell through the entrance. The duckboards squelched on a bed of mud and the deck chairs were damp. We huddled together and Mavis whispered, "Make a hand swandwich with me, Lil?" But I pretended I didn't hear her. Mum pestered Grandad to let her run back and make a thermos of cocoa. Grandad said no one was leaving the shelter, something big was going on. He kept going outside nevertheless and coming back with reports of aircraft going over in layers, following the line of the river, ignoring the flank, saving their bombs for some other objective.

"Poor old London again, I suppose," Mum said wearily.

"Don't be daft, girl. They'd be peeling off to the east then, wouldn't they? I thought it might be the city docks. Or the railway marshaling yards. But they're going on. Birmingham or Crewe."

"In that case, let's get back inside before we all die of pneumonia," Mum snapped.

"Not bloody likely." Grandad wasn't going to risk any of us dropping off to sleep and missing this. "You never know when they might start unloading. We're safe here."

"Mavis wants to go to the can."

"That's nothing unusual. You've got a chamber pot in the corner."

There was a lot of fuss while we disrobed Mavis in the dark and sat her on the pot. Meanwhile Grandad disappeared completely outside.

When he came back Mum's temper was in tatters.

"You went back to the house to use the toilet," she said frigidly, trying to show her displeasure by posh words.

"Talking about it made me want to go," Grandad explained, still doing up his fly while trying to look back down on the city.

"You're enjoying this whole thing," Mum accused furiously. "You're like a kid playing at soldiers —"

"Look here, Grace. I promised Albert —"

I don't know what happened. Goodness knows I was used to their bickering. It was part of my life. I didn't even realize it was me . . . I listened to the screams . . . heard Mum shouting at me . . . felt Grandad's horny hand as he slapped my face . . . wondered dreamily what all the fuss was about.

But as that thin screaming went on and on I knew with awful certainty that the war wasn't happening outside. It had come right into our midst.

CHAPTER
EIGHT

We heard on the wireless the next day that Coventry had "got it." Mum, who had visited a favorite aunt there as a child, leaned over the wireless set with blind eyes, remembering.

"The three spires are still there," she reported to Grandad, smiling somehow. "They couldn't finish it off completely."

Her grief about Coventry was somehow bound up with her anxiety for me. She made me a bed on the sofa where I could stare blankly up the track and recall my stupid Warsaw game of a year ago — how young I had been — and she sent for Doctor Burns.

"Bowels all right?" he asked briskly, shoving a thermometer under my tongue and taking my pulse. I nodded and Mum said, "Well . . ." and he glanced at his wristwatch and went on, "Sickness? Off food? Irritation?"

I shook my head, and Mum said determinedly, "Her appetite has been very poor lately, Doctor. And of course without any oranges in the shops her vitamin C intake —" Mum liked to show that she was up on all the latest things.

He said, "Send her to Nanny Dexter's for a spoonful of her black currants." He looked at the thermometer and shook it down. "Could you rinse this for me, Mrs. Freeman." He waited till Mum went into the kitchen and said, "New school getting you down, Lily?"

Tears rushed into my eyes and I nodded.

He gripped my wrist very hard. "Any news of your dad?"

"He's been sent somewhere. We don't know where yet."

"Hm. And you're missing your cousin, of course." He heaved a sigh. "Nothing I can do for you, lass. Except give you a medical certificate for a couple of weeks at home. What are the school meals like?"

"We have potatoes boiled in their skins," I whispered. "And we have to eat the skins."

"Good. That's where the food value is." He rubbed my wrist. "Pretend Nanny cooked 'em and they'll be delicious." He ruminated, grunting like Grandad. "Maybe you could go and see your cousin during your midday break, Lily? Is that possible?"

"If I took my bike —" My heart lifted slightly.

"Well then. And spend a night there too occasionally. It will ease the strain." He stood up. "You know your old schoolmaster would help you with your work if you asked him. And if you don't want to tell your mother about the school, Nanny Dexter would listen. Or have you outgrown Nanny?"

I shook my head. Two weeks at home. The curtain between me and my norm moved aside slightly. Mr. Edwards . . . Nanny . . . and even when I had to go back, there could be Phil every dinnertime.

Very, very slowly things improved. Mum and I spent a lot of that two weeks knitting blanket squares for Coventry; I visited Nan and Mr. Edwards; we took the bus and went down to Lake Cottage. My world began to take shape around me and I wouldn't take it for granted again. Fleetingly I wondered about Mum; but after all she still had Grandad.

Christmas came and a letter from Dad too. He still couldn't say where he was, but Grandad and Mum reckoned it was Africa, where Grandad said we were "dusting up the Eyeties." Grandad took us into the village hall and showed us the war map on the wall with the little Union Jack flags in small — very small — clusters here and there.

In April the German planes came over again in the same layered formation and had another go at Coventry. By this time we had given up using the air-raid shelter, and I lay in bed gabbling my usual prayer over and over as if it were a lucky charm. "Please, God, don't let the Germans drop any bombs on us. Please, God, keep Dad safe in Africa. Please, God, guard over Aunt Florrie and Phil and Uncle Bert. Please, God, don't let the Germans . . ." God listened but somehow when we heard the news on the wireless the next day I felt guilty. I had been granted my prayer at a terrible cost to someone else.

Then it was the summer term and there was tennis and unexpectedly I found something I could do well. I played a girl called Erica Lorimer and won the Junior Cup for Kyneburgh House. Miss Crail put her arm around my shoulders and hugged me, and Mum, Grandad, Aunt Flo, and Phil sat in the visitors' stands and beamed brighter than the sun.

Later, Phil and I took our tea outside into the garden at Lake Cottage and I tried to explain about tennis. Her eyes never left my face.

"Phil . . ." It was so difficult to know just how much Philippa really understood. ". . . You are happy down here, aren't you? Now that I come to see you every day and sleep with you on Wednesday nights —" She nodded vigorously. "Only you never seem to go out anywhere — you sort of hide away here. Aunt Flo says you won't go for a walk with her like you used to in the hills."

"Go my school," she said. "See my Lily."

I didn't want to worry about Phil. I didn't want to worry about Mum — or Dad. I'd only just emerged from a fog of misery about myself; I didn't want to worry about anything else.

"Listen," I said. "I've just thought of a poem." I swung Phil's hands in time to the meter and chanted, "Quickly and quietly, Erica Lorimer, run down to Warsaw and fetch me some guns. Quickly and quietly, Erica Lorimer, run down to Warsaw, watch out for Huns."

We rolled on the grass laughing foolishly and then we played hide-and-seek in the thick foliage of the soft-fruit enclosure.

Going home in GY with the windows down and my sandals on the seat, I asked Mum, "Was I christened Lily or Lillian?"

"Lily. After the flower." She glanced over her shoulder at me. "Why?"

"Lillian goes better. 'I'm Lily Freeman of Kyneburgh House' sounds daft. But Lillian is all right. I'll be Lillian from now on." I shouted into the glowing evening, "I'm Lillian Freeman of Kyneburgh House!"

There was a letter waiting from Dad. Mum read it and told me he'd sent his love and then put it in her bag. I went to bed, but it wasn't dark and I couldn't sleep, so about ten-thirty I went down to see if Mum was making cocoa. Halfway down the stairs I heard her crying.

Grandad's voice said, "There now, Grace. Once he gets back home it'll be all right. Don't take on so."

Something stopped me from charging into the living room. I stayed where I was, frozen to the spot.

Mum sounded as though she was choking on her own tears.

"It's never been all right. You know that better than anyone. He'd have never married me if it hadn't been for Lil. Oh God. What am I going to *do*?"

"Go on living quietly. This ruddy war will end soon and he'll come home —"

"Dad — he says he's giving me my freedom! And this house is yours — what good is freedom when there's nowhere to go!" Her voice rose in a wail unlike anything I'd heard before from Mum.

"Don't be daft, Grace. This is your home. Whatever Albert does or says, you're my daughter-in-law and Lily's my grandchild." He grunted a snort. "Besides. How the hell could I look after myself, what with rations and all?"

There was a hiatus in Mum's crying. Then she snuffled a small attempt at a laugh.

"Trust you to bring things down to earth, Dad," she said. She sounded almost normal. There was another pause, a long one, punctuated by her blowing her nose and Grandad grunting and the sudden heart-stopping eleven-o'clock chimes on the clock. I felt with my heel for the next step up.

Mum said fiercely, "I've still got Lily. I've still got her." Another grunt. "I shan't tell her about her father — you mustn't mention it either, Dad. We can pretend his leaves are canceled or something — he'll go on writing to her, he's sure to. You won't say anything, Dad —"

"No. All right. It's best that way."

There was the faintest sound above me and I jerked around convulsively and met Mavis' eyes above the landing banisters. For a brief second we stared at each other and I knew that she had heard . . . enough. The ends of her mouth turned up slightly in her small smile and she turned and scuttled back to her room.

Slowly and cautiously I crept back to mine. Mum and me. Just Mum and me. That's how it had always been. But now that I knew why, our togetherness felt different. Weighty. Almost like a responsibility.

CHAPTER
NINE

That summer Mavis went on a special camp organized by Little Dorrit for the evacuees, so Grandad and Mum and Aunt Flo and Phil and I took the train to Cornwall for two whole weeks. We booked at a marvelous place; a townlet on a peninsula with beaches either side of it. Sand was everywhere, in all our clothes and most of our food, down our ears, under our finger- and toenails, even *inside* our pillow slips. Our landlady, Mrs. Hoskins, couldn't get over it.

The sea was even older than our hills and had as many moods. I loved to listen to it before I slept and hear it again with my first waking thought and know that it had been going on while I was somewhere else, like a guardian. The waves were strong and I was a weak swimmer, so I was quite content to splash with Phil in the shallows. We resumed our old easy friendship, with me the leader and Phil the willing, stumbling shadow highlighting my expertise by her ineptitude. Sometimes I missed Ron and Freda; then I wasn't always kind to Phil; then I was guilty.

At the weekend we were in our usual picnic spot on the beach when we spotted a khaki-colored car bumping along the sandy track that led to the town.

"Who on earth can this be?" wondered Mum, shading her eyes with a long honey-colored hand. "More convalescent soldiers?" Grandad liked to visit the one or two wheelchairs parked along the sand for a chat and a pipe; he grunted hopefully.

Aunt Flo stood up, holding on to her big straw hat against the breeze coming off the Atlantic.

"D'you know, I do believe . . . it is . . . Bert!"

She started to run and we all joined her. It was indeed Uncle Bert driving the official car. Another man sat in the passenger seat; lanky and very blond, his shirt open at the neck like a cricketer. He inhibited our first rush of questions and Uncle Bert could explain.

"An American visitor." He introduced us without formality. "Mr. Bob Critchley, who is going to join our backroom boys." He grinned at Mr. Critchley, quite at home. "Bob is a boffin, a scientist. He thinks America will be in the war quite soon and he wants to be first over here." Mr. Critchley grinned back easily, not like a boffin at all. But Americans were different, of course. "Bob — my family. From left to right. Mr. Freeman senior, known to everyone as Dad. Grace, Florrie, Phil, Lily." He opened the rear doors invitingly and Phil and I swarmed inside. The car was twice as big as GY.

Uncle Bert went on while Phil wound her arms around him from behind.

"They wanted Bob to see a bit of the place before he started on his new inventions —"

Mr. Critchley said something. It might have been shucks.

"— so I thought — why not this little corner of the old place? Where it so happens we run into my nearest and dearest — pure coincidence of course —"

Aunt Florrie said, "Oh, Bert, you never change, do you?"

"You are incorrigible," I said from the backseat, longing to air my new word.

Mum said, "Lil, you little show-off!"

Uncle Bert said, "It's true. I am . . . whatever you said, Lil."

Bob Critchley said, "It was my idea, Mrs . . . okay, okay, Bert, Florrie, it is. And I'm Bob. Seriously, we had to visit Plymouth and Bert was telling me about this little place and I said — why not spend the weekend there?"

"So here we are." Uncle Bert carefully unwound Phil's arms. "Jump in, everyone, and show us the digs. Lily, climb over and sit between us — Christ, mind my ear. Did you ever see such long legs, Bob?"

"Never," said Mr. Critchley with great conviction. "Not even on Betty Grable."

I wriggled down between them wondering if it was a compliment.

Uncle Bert slammed doors and said, "Plenty of room, eh? You all right, Grace? Any news of Albert?"

I rushed in fast. "I've had a letter. There's half a page that's been blue-penciled so it must have said where he was —"

"Censored, not blue-penciled, Lily."

"Blue pencil" was becoming a sort of innocuous swear world. There was a comedian on the wireless who used it a lot, and when I'd told Grandad to look at my "blue-pencil sand castle" he'd roared laughing.

Uncle Bert started up the engine and tapped his nose.

"I've heard things on the grapevine. There's going to be something big out in Africa. That's what Albert was trying to tell you, I'll be bound."

We roared opulently along the deserted road. Mrs. Hoskins hadn't had visitors since the war started and she treated us like royalty. Uncle Bert put the finishing touches to everything by kissing her hand.

"A little break — a welcome break — from the rigors of war, dear lady. That is what you offer here."

"I had no idea you were a military gentleman," fluttered Mrs. Hoskins, completely ignoring Mr. Critchley.

"I am what is known as a backroom boy, dear lady. A scientist if you prefer. I am not in the front line like my brother-in-law, but the strains are, nevertheless, very great."

"I saw a film," Mrs. Hoskins said eagerly. "Leslie Howard was in it. It was called *The First of the Few* —"

"Exactly. However, we mustn't talk about it." Uncle Bert smiled his devastating smile and used a phrase from the billboards with sidesplitting solemnity, "Be like Dad. Keep Mum. Eh?"

Mum held my hand warningly, though she was quivering with laughter herself, but Aunt Florrie frowned and hustled Uncle Bert into unloading the car.

Uncle Bert was in his element. He had Bob — he was immediately Bob to all of us — and Grandad as drinking companions, and his "beautiful women" now included Mum and me. He liked to chase us along the beach in front of the other few holiday-makers; if we were in the sea, we had to be dunked; if we were on the sand, we had to be buried.

On Sunday afternoon Bob had taken Phil for a swimming lesson and Aunt Flo was trying to unpack our tea in the shelter of a deck chair.

Uncle Bert said, "Not more sand sandwiches? Why don't we skip tea and go out for a meal this evening?"

"Because a cooked meal at night upsets Phil and she's sick," explained Aunt Flo carefully. "Is she all right with your American, Bert?"

"Is he all right with her, you mean."

"All right, that is what I meant. You should teach her to swim, Bert. You're her father."

Uncle Bert picked up the newspaper and put it over his eyes.

"Bob doesn't mind. If I can get a permanent job as his driver, I'll be in clover."

"You take advantage of him. Driving all down here — you knew how far it was —"

"They never *use* the blue-pencil car." He lifted the paper and winked at me. "And they've got enough petrol to drive a bus to Berlin and back. Don't worry so, Florrie, for God's sake."

"You'll go too far, Bert. First the black-market silk stockings and now this —"

He flung aside the paper and sat up. He looked at Aunt Flo and spoke to Mum.

"D'you know, Grace, your sister is becoming the world's best nagger. First she wants what she calls a proper home. So I rent the best house in Gloucester and she grumbles at me for paying for it with silk stockings. Then she doesn't want to go on holiday because I can't come and when I turn up —"

Aunt Florrie dropped an egg sandwich into the sand and said in a high voice, "I'm only worried in case you get caught, Bert. I don't think I could bear it if you were put inside again!"

Mum said, "Come on, Lil. Let's go for a paddle."

Uncle Bert said, "I appreciate your concern, my dear. But sometimes it . . . smothers me!"

As Mum pulled me down to the sea, laughing gaily to cover the sound of their raised voices, I looked up at her and thought what a lot there was went on that children never knew about. It was kept from us in the name of love.

I felt a queer sympathy for Uncle Bert.

Bob helped me with my swimming too and taught me not to be afraid of the rollers.

"They're babies compared with the ones back home," he said as he waded into them with me clinging to his back like a limpet. "Either use them or let them roll over you. Pinch your nose, Lil — go on — now just sit on the bottom and wait till it's gone."

We went down together and I forgot to close my eyes. Above us the bottom side of the wave was the same as the top view without the spray and noise and fear. I came up laughing.

"Like Grandad when he stops grunting and fuming," I said and though Bob had known Grandad only two days he understood and laughed.

I was sorry when they left. But I didn't want to go with them.

Two days later we were splashing in the shallows when the tide was out. Mum and Aunt Florrie were in deck chairs, tiny silhouettes on the almost empty beach. Grandad was keeping watch for the beer truck, which was due that day with the local allocation of beer. The sky was high and cloudless, and I'd invented a new game that Phil and I were part of an invasion force in Africa. Every now and then we had to duck to avoid gunfire — I'd read in Ron's comic that bullets ricocheted on water. It was great fun.

Over the horizon two dots appeared. I watched them knowledgeably.

"Spitfires," I told Phil. "Returning from —" They rolled lazily over the beach and objects fell from their bellies. "Lummy," I yelped. "Those are blue-pencil parachutes!"

The parachutes dropped like stones; there were almighty explosions and the town on the peninsula was enveloped in orange flame. I stared at it, then stupidly at Philippa.

"They were bombs," I said between stiff lips.

Philippa stared back at me, her face expressing only astonishment. Then the planes appeared from the pall of black smoke which crowned that orange flame. They swept low over the beach and spurts of sand followed them.

"They're shooting!" I screamed. "Phil, they're trying to kill us!" I looked toward the tiny silhouettes on the beach and they had gone. "Mum!" I shrieked at the top of my voice, all control vanished. "Mum — Mum — Mum —"

A hand came across my mouth. I looked up into Phil's face. It was full of concern. No fear, no panic, just concern. The hand dragged me down into the knee-deep sea. The long body was on top of me protecting me. The planes roared again overhead and water spurted irritably around us.

"Mum!" I screamed. "Mum — please — Mum —"

"Phil's here . . . Phil's here, Lily . . . Phil's here . . ." The voice crooned on beneath my hysterical shrieks. I gulped a breath and stared beyond her large head. The planes were zooming over the headland and banking in a turn. The oily black smoke covered the beach and rolled toward us. The planes began their run again and I gasped despairingly, "Oh, God — they're coming again, Phil . . . oh, God —"

Phil smiled her wide smile.

"Under the water now, Lily? Under now?"

Did she think we were still playing our game? Engine roar filled the world and I remembered — just — to snatch some air before going under. Again I didn't remember to close my eyes; Phil's face was inches from mine, her hair floating up like seaweed, her smile ridiculous in the crystal clear water. We stuck it as long as we could, then surfaced. The smoke was all around us, the sky gone. Mum and Aunt Florrie sounded like angels. "Lily!" "Phil!"

Then they were holding us and we were weeping.

The smoke cleared eventually and we trailed back up the beach. A legless soldier, recuperating, was helpless on his back, blown out of his wheelchair by the blast. We found his chair and got him back in; he was gasping with the pain from inside his pinned-up trouser legs. Somehow we wheeled him through the sand. Our own deck chairs and picnic things were nowhere to be seen — we never found them. Our favorite dresses that Aunt Florrie had made a year ago were gone forever though, as Aunt Flo said, they were getting a bit short in the knee. And we were safe. If they told us that once they told us a hundred times: as we walked the sandy road to

Mrs. Hoskins' — no window glass and two ceilings down; as we made tea on a Primus and took it to her in bed because she was suffering from shock and there was no gas because one of the bombs had hit the gas holder; as we discovered that Grandad couldn't stand up, not because of injury but because a broken whisky bottle had dripped into his mouth when he took shelter beneath the bar . . . they kept telling us.

I wept again because there was glass in my bed and I cut my toe on it.

"What does it matter, darling?" Mum soothed, plastering my foot with lint and antiseptic. "Just as long as we're safe. All safe together."

That night Aunt Florrie had a terrible time with Philippa. She wailed until Mrs. Hoskins wailed with her. Nothing could placate her. We had a wide-eyed conference around her bed while Mrs. Hoskins shouted at us to shut her up.

"It's delayed shock," Mum said soothingly. "She can't bear violence and she just realizes what's happened."

"She's a loony!" shouted Mrs. Hoskins. "I knew immediately I saw her. That husband of yours soft-soaped me, and that Yank — I bet he was a spy — and now a loony is going to tear us all to shreds!"

I don't remember hitting her, only Mum dragging me off her. She was spread-eagled against the wall, her eyes black with horror.

"Two of them!" she gasped. And she opened the door and ran.

I clambered into bed with Phil and got inside her flailing arms. I didn't have to feign my tears.

"Phil . . . I'm frightened . . . so frightened . . ." I whimpered as she paused to take breath. The wailing lessened slightly and her arms held me. "Phil. Let me stay with you. Please let me stay . . ."

Gradually she calmed. Mum and Aunt Florrie sat quietly by the bed and I wept against the baggy cotton nightie and remembered my old Warsaw dreams of killing Jerries and being brave.

At last she slept and I slid out of her bed and went back to my own. Mum tucked me in.

"You and Philippa . . . I didn't realize you were so close," she said hesitantly, as if she might be intruding on something private.

"Neither did I." I looked at her with dry eyes, my face so stiff it pained. "Mum . . . Phil loves me better than herself. That's why . . . that's why . . ." She hugged me and I shook like the aspens in the field at home. "Mum," I gasped out. "She saved my life today."

"I know. I know, chookie . . ."

"Mum . . . she's brave. Really brave."

"Yes, Lily. She's really brave."

The next morning Mrs. Hoskins asked us to leave. We packed and caught a slow train. The weather had broken and it rained incessantly. Aunt Florrie got out at Plymouth and telephoned Lake Cottage, but there was no reply, so we took a taxi when we got to Gloucester. There was no milk in the house and it was too late to buy bread or anything else. We opened a box of biscuits left over from Christmas and made drinks with bouillon and went to bed.

Aunt Flo said wearily, "It's no good you keep looking on the bright side, Grace. He hasn't even been home. He must have gone straight to that woman."

Mum said, "Be fair, Flo. You don't know that. He might have gone to Bob's digs —"

Aunt Flo didn't argue. She said, "Oh, what's the use?"

Was growing up simply a process of discovering that security was insecure and that infallibility was always supremely fallible? For the rest of that summer I immersed myself in the life of the hills; I was ringleader in a dozen escapades; I played fiercely in an effort to shut out the suspicion that the Jerries were almost an adjunct to my war. In fact there were times when I thought of them with a sneaking gratitude as something to pin my fears and hates on.

Philippa came to stay with us while Uncle Bert and Aunt Florrie had a holiday by themselves to "sort things out," and I invented a game based on our experience in Cornwall that involved Ron, Freda, Dennis, Audrey, Mavis, Phil, and me immersing ourselves at regular intervals in our stream. It was gloriously hot and the plum harvest was rich. Starved of sweetness, we gorged on the cracked and dripping plums, washing away the stickiness every time someone screamed, "Enemy planes!" It was great fun and helped me to forget my craven fear that day. I don't know whether Phil even remembered her case of "delayed shock" and our nice Mrs. Hoskins suddenly turning very nasty. I wrote about it to Dad in the form of an epic poem in the hope of avoiding the censorious blue pencil, but he never mentioned it in his replies so perhaps "they" thought it was a code.

So school started again. We did German that year as well as French, and our new mistress was called Miss Field.

Miss Field was a dark, handsome woman, big and lumbering with threads of gray in her Eton crop, thick stockings, brogues, a beautiful deep voice. Her courtesy reminded me of Mr. Edwards, but she was older than he was and could remember the world before the First World War when she had studied at Heidelberg. Her Germany had nothing to do with Nazis and everything to do with castles on the Rhine, Geothe's poetry, Strauss waltzes and Lederhosen. The German room was half in the eaves and had dormer windows and some of the original school desks. Sitting in one of them tracing ridges in the wood with my thumbnail, I came across some familiar initials. G.O.O. Grace Olivia Oxendale. There couldn't be anyone else with such crazy initials. It was Mum.

A year ago that would have meant everything to me.

Just after half-term, when I was thirteen and three weeks old, the bell rang for an emergency assembly and we gathered in the high domed hall and watched Doctor Pensford apprehensively as she flapped to her lectern like a crow in her black gown.

She smiled at us as usual, her stony eyes going along the ranks for anything out of place.

"I expect most of you heard the news before you left home this morning. The British Eighth Army has started an offensive in North Africa and I think it only right that we should have a short service to ask protection for our soldiers. And a half day this afternoon —"

The rest of her announcement was lost in murmurs of excitement and then the head girl suddenly sang out, "Three cheers for our army in Africa. Hip-hip . . ."

We cheered frantically to cover our previous interruption. Doctor Pensford was quite capable of immediately withdrawing the half day. She barely waited for the echoes to die away before commanding, "Please attend, girls. I have another announcement to make. You will have noticed that Ursula Cunningforth has not been with us since the half-term holiday." The eyes looked beyond us at the roll of honor. "She has been expelled from the high school for behavior unfitting to our standards. Let us pray."

We all knelt in a ferment of speculation. I tried to think of Dad, who might well be taking part in the "offensive" in Africa, but I had a job to remember his face. Whereas Ursula Cunningforth's was all too clear.

The Crypt had a half day, too, so Miss Crail drove us home and talked to Ron about the war as if he were grown up. Her underlip kept catching on her wonky tooth and Ron leaned forward adoringly and said that if we could drive the Axis powers out of Eritrea it would do morale a lot of good.

Freda waited her chance and then gasped, "Miss Crail, why has Ursula been expelled? She wasn't even a scholarship girl."

It was a well-known fact that fee-paying girls were more upright and honest than scholarship girls.

Miss Crail looked at us in the driving mirror, a long considering look.

"Listen, girls. It'll be all over the school by Christmas so you might as well know the truth of it. Ursula is having a baby."

Freda and I were winded, physically. Ron was intensely embarrassed.

Miss Crail went on into the silence, "Don't let it upset you — you're very young but I expect you know it happens sometimes. When girls are foolish and let themselves be blinded by what they call love." She sighed. "Ursula's parents have been generous and opened their doors to a number of foreign soldiers . . . I believe it is a Canadian . . ."

Freda whispered, "How awful. How awful. I'd kill myself — I couldn't face it — "

"Don't be silly, Freda." Miss Crail tried to be brisk now but she couldn't obliterate her previous disgust. "Ursula will have the baby adopted, I daresay, and do some worthwhile work later on."

There was another silence. Below us on the road a convoy of tanks crawled by; the fields on either side of us were dark and wet after the turnip crop, the trees leafless. I thought of Ursula, disgraced forever. Like Freda, I knew there was only one solution to such a problem.

It was beginning to get dark as I wandered down the track, and Gloucester, in spite of the blackout, was beginning to glow quietly in the November fog below. There was no sign of Mum or Mavis in the living room; I was much earlier than usual, of course. I dumped my satchel, gaberdine, and school velour in the hall and started up the stairs. Grandad's bedroom door opened and . . . Mrs. Willis came out and hurried down toward me.

I was astonished. As far as I knew Mrs. Willis had never been in our house before. I said stupidly, "Freda's already at home. We had a half day because of the new attack in Africa."

She paused momentarily to take this in, then said in Freda's whisper, "Oh . . . Lily . . ." Then she came on down the rest of the stairs and bundled me into the living room. "Freda will be all right. Mr. Willis is there. I didn't want to leave your poor mother."

"Mum?" My heart was squeezed. "She's ill?"

"No, my dear. She's bearing up remarkably well. Remarkably." Mrs. Willis did not look pleased. "I sent Mavis to our place. Freda will look after her tonight."

I stared at her, fascinated by a mole on her chin sprouting hairs. Did Freda ever giggle with this woman like I did with Mum?

She patted my hand. "Poor child. You'll miss him, I know. But it was a kind and wonderful way to go. Feeding his poultry, having a drink with the Home Guard, walking home as usual and then —"

"Grandad? What's happened to Grandad?"

"Mr. Willis was driving the trap down to Crake's to fetch the pig food, and he was in the road. Already gone."

"*Dead?*" My voice was harsh and unbelieving. "He can't be *dead*!"

"It's a shock, my dear. I'll make you some tea in a minute —"

"But is he dead, Mrs. Willis? Grandad — is he dead?"

"We prefer the term 'passed over' in chapel, my dear. If you think of it as a curtain dividing this life from another —"

"He can't be! I don't believe it. Nan said none of my family — none of them —" I got up from the armchair where she had so gently shoved me and darted into the hall. "It isn't true!" I was halfway up the stairs, and she was calling urgently, "Lily — come back, child. You don't want to —" But I was already at his door, lifting it slightly to get it over the threadbare carpet, smelling the familiar smell of pipe tobacco and . . . something else. Disinfectant?

A sheet covered him completely so that I should have known, but nothing would have stopped me then. I pulled it back just as Mum came into the room behind me.

"Lily —"

A great cry came from me. A physical thing, emanating from my whole body, hoarse and ugly, filling Grandad's room. I half fell over the bed, my legs giving way beneath me. He lay there, pennies on his eyes, his white quiff of hair brushed neatly back from his forehead, his hands crossed on the chest of a nightshirt. Mrs. Willis was known throughout the district for her beautiful laying out, and Grandad looked exactly as he had looked in life.

Except that he wasn't there.

It was my first sight of human death. For me it was just that. The absence of life. And it was unbelievable. This morning Grandad had inhabited this body. And now he did not. I wanted to scurridge around the bedroom looking for him except for the remnant of logic that told me clearly what had happened.

Mum gathered me up and turned my head into her neck. We got ourselves onto the landing — past the tutting Mrs. Willis, who went into the bedroom to check on her handiwork — down the stairs, and into the living room again. We sat together on the sofa, hanging on to one another still. I tried to cry, forcing out childish sobs, blubbering to fill in the gap, the silence, the abyss. Mum said, "There, there, Lil. He's all right. Don't worry, darling, he's all right." And then suddenly she said, "Poor old Dad

. . . poor old Dad . . ." and I cried in earnest because she was crying.

Little Dorrit was marvelous and superintended the funeral arrangements and ran us down to register his death. Aunt Florrie and Phil came to stay. Mr. Edwards called several times. Uncle Bert walked with Mum behind the coffin, Aunt Flo and me next. The Home Guard was there in uniform and so were some of Dad's old colleagues from the railway office.

The next day I went to see Nanny Dexter.

"You told me no one in my family would die," I accused her immediately as I opened the door into the firelit dimness of her kitchen. "I believed you. And Grandad is dead."

She looked up. In the last year she had changed; her frail skeleton was plainly visible pushing out the tortoise skin; her hat looked several sizes too big for her.

She said, "Lily, I've been expecting you." She leaned her head against the patchwork cushion. "Did they all turn out for him? Was it a good funeral?"

I was sickened. "You made it up. You made it all up. You can't see into the future at all."

She said vaguely, "Past and future, 'tis all one. Your grandad did have a good life, Lily. Remember that." She pushed at the fireplace screen with the toe of her boot. "Get yourself a potato, girl, and sit down. You're getting that tall I can't see you a-standing there —"

"You knew about Mum having to get married, didn't you? That's why she didn't like me listening to your tales — you knew about her!"

"Your mam?" The hooded eyes met mine. "Ah. So someone's told you, have they? Freda is it? 'Tis old history, Lily, make no mistake about it —"

"More lies!" I was shaking all over. "It isn't old history at all. It's why Mum's still a foreigner and why Dad's not coming back and perhaps even — perhaps why Grandad dropped down dead before his time!" I turned from her abruptly. "I'm not coming here again. D'you hear me? I'm not coming here again!"

She said nothing. I waited at the door for something — some crumb to make everything all right again. It didn't come. I slammed the door.

The willows drooped soddenly around the pond. I remembered the day I had crouched in one, sped on my way by Grandad.

"You didn't even say good-bye to me," I said angrily to the empty land. "And now Mum's on her own. Really on her own."

Because — knowing what I knew now — how could I help her?

I thought of Ursula Cunningforth, and I knew quite clearly what I would have done.

A lone goose honked overhead sounding strangely like our old car. And even more strangely like Grandad.

CHAPTER
TEN

Bob took us out to dinner to celebrate the fact that we were allies. When Uncle Bert cracked a joke about Pearl Harbor, he didn't laugh much but apart from that it was what he called "quite a party." There was a band in a palm-fringed alcove and they played a song called "Mr. Franklin D. Roosevelt Jones" that I recognized as a quick-step.

"Do you dance, Lil?" Bob asked in his lovely drawl.

Aunt Flo said quickly, "Of course she does. Go on, Lil — just once around the floor."

I shook my head, feeling my face go warm. "I can only do the three-quarter turn, Bob. That's as far as we've got at school."

"Then we'll three-quarter turn all around the whole darn place. Will you do me the honor, ma'am?" He got up and sketched a funny bow and I giggled and Aunt Flo pushed me upright and Phil clapped her hands.

Somehow, like a cat on hot bricks, I got around the room. Bob swung my hand and sang the lyrics at me but I couldn't relax. I knew my face was bright red, my blouse was pulling out of my skirt, my freshly curled hair was drooping on one side. If only it had been different — I had been different — so that I could tell Freda and maybe Erica Lorimer of my prowess the next day.

Bob said, "Say, you're doing fine, honey. But if you're trying to show me up as a raw, jitterbugging Yank, I promise I won't speak to you for a month."

I met his eyes, my own agonized. "I wish I could jitterbug . . . I wish I could dance properly. Oh damn . . . start again please, Bob. Slow, quick, quick, slow . . ."

We zigzagged on a little more easily.

"Honest, Lil, you're marvelous. I'm getting the hang of it now —"

"Oh, Bob, you could do it all the time!"

"I swear to God, honey, your English dancing is a closed book to me."

"Bob *Critchley* —"

"Lily *Freeman*." We grinned at each other more naturally. Then he lifted me and held me against his chest and did some very fancy footwork. As we passed our table Phil and Aunt Flo clapped. He put me down sedately.

"I wish you'd stop showing off, Lil. Honestly."

I danced automatically within the circle of his arm, gasping with laughter.

"It was like flying, Bob. Oh, Bob . . . you really are *good*. Could you teach me to dance properly? At school we never do anything like that."

He opened his very blue eyes in pretended amazement.

"Aw come on, Lil. You know I can't dance."

Phil watched us wonderingly when we moved the sitting-room furniture and practiced our dance steps. Bob made her stand up and have a go, too, but her legs wouldn't do what she told them to and she preferred to watch. He congratulated me, pulling my earlobe and telling me I had a good sense of rhythm. Then he put his big hand on Phil's hair.

"And you watch better than anyone I know, Phil," he said. "It's important to watch. And listen. I've seen you sitting by the piano and soaking up the music." He glanced at me. "D'you like music, Lily? Proper music?"

"Classical?" I made a face. "We have to listen at school. It's a bit boring."

He went to the piano and lifted the lid. "I haven't played since I left home. It makes me homesick. But just for you ladies . . ." He flexed his fingers over the keys. Very gently the tentative arpeggios of the "Moonlight Sonata" dropped into the room. Phil crept to the floor and sat in between the piano legs. I watched, astonished.

At the end I said, "You never told us. You're a proper pianist and you never said a word."

His eyes were far away. His fingers wandered over the keyboard finding chords, listening carefully to them.

"I'm no pianist — no professional, Lily. It's . . . math and music often go together."

"Math?"

"I'm a mathematician. I came over here to make bomb-aiming devices." He smiled quickly at me.

113

"Let me be honest for once. I came over here to get away from the life I was leading, Lil. A lot of men go to war for that reason."

I thought fleetingly of Dad. But it was Bob who interested me.

"Are you married then, Bob?" It was a vital question for some reason. I held my breath.

The smile widened. "Lil, you're growing up fast. That's a question most women ask at some time or another. No, honey, I didn't quite get to the altar." He pounded into a song Aunt Flo and Uncle Bert sang — "Waiting at the Church."

I said suddenly without stopping to consider, "My dad isn't coming back to us. So you're not the only one . . . left in the lurch."

He stopped playing. His hands stayed poised over the keys and he started at them, keeping very still.

Phil said, "Play again . . . play again . . ."

His fingers began to move again. More arpeggios. "Für Elise." He said softly, "That is why . . . Is that why Grace is lonely?"

I shrugged. "Not only that. Grandad. And other things, too."

"I see." The fingers searched for chords and found them. He said, "After the war . . . he'll come back, of course."

"He doesn't love us. He never did. I don't know."

"Oh, Lil . . ." He bent his head for a moment then looked up at me, his blue eyes angry. "Of course he loves you. Don't talk like that again. He loves you. Understand?"

114

I didn't answer immediately and he came to the end of his piece, paused for the vibrations to die, and then gently closed the piano lid.

"Understand, Lily?" he repeated quietly.

"Yes."

"Good girl." He spun around on the piano stool and touched Phil. "What did you think of my music, Flippa? Was it boring?"

I protested, "I wasn't bored. Honestly, Bob. I wasn't."

Phil rocked gently. "More music, Bob. More."

"Next time, honey. Maybe I'll take your musical education in hand. After one of our crazy dancing lessons, it will do you good to listen to Beethoven."

"Yes please, Bob. We should like that."

He stood up and pulled Phil to her feet. "You don't have to be polite, honey. Let's go and see what your Aunt Flo has to eat . . ."

I wasn't being polite. How could I tell him what his music had done for me? How could I explain that for the first time his fairness looked Nordic to me . . . that beneath his English pullover his shoulders seemed definitely American, very square and a little hunched.

That spring I was measured at school for extra clothing coupons because I was taller than average. Mum sewed suspenders on the end of my liberty bodice so that I could start wearing stockings. Bob said I had better legs than Betty Grable.

At half-term the weather was shocking, and Mavis had a rasping cough to go with her running nose.

"I'll fetch Doc Burns, shall I, Mum?" I suggested after our breakfast eggs. We still had Grandad's hens, of course.

"Not in this weather. You've outgrown your Wellingtons and you'll get your feet soaking."

"I think he ought to come and see Mavis." I looked at her doubtfully. It was impossible to tell how ill she really was; she could wheeze and cough at will. "Besides he might give us a permit for some extra coal."

"They wouldn't deliver it. No, don't get wet for nothing, chookie. I can wrap Mavis up and dose her with Gee's linctus."

I went into the kitchen where Grandad's Wellingtons still stood by the back door. He hadn't been a big man and they were a size eight — I already took a six.

"I can stuff paper in these, Mum. They'll do. I want to ask Freda about the math homework, anyway."

She stood by the window watching me anxiously. She seemed always anxious now.

Doctor Burns came and gave us a prescription for some more Gee's linctus and a permit for coal. Also some vitamin tablets for Mum. I cycled to the station where Elliot's coal yard burgeoned from the siding like a giant wart.

"If we ain't got no coal we can't deliver it, permit nor no bleeding permit," Mr. Elliot said sulkily.

"You've got coal. I can see it." My anger was somehow connected with guilt.

"That's the railway coal as you should know, my girl. And less of the lip. If there's one thing I can't stand it's lippy kids."

"I'm not a kid. And we're entitled to railway coal. I'll write to the general manager and point out that my father is fighting for his country and our registered coal-man refuses to —"

"You ain't got that much nerve."

"It doesn't take nerve. Just an ability to write a letter."

"Bloody little snob. All you Freemans is the same." He got off his high stool and grumbled his way into the yard. "This lot's gotta do for the rest of the winter, I'll have you know. I could let you have two or three hundred next week —"

"Thank you, Mr. Elliot." I summoned up a smile. "I'll take half a hundredweight now. If you don't mind."

"How? The horse is out —"

"I've got my bike." I was amazed and pleased with myself. Nothing could stand in my way. Until I took the weight of the sack on my bike frame — then I wondered how on earth I would get home. Mr. Elliot took the trouble to come outside and watch me stagger off, a sardonic smile on his face. My nails broke as I hung on to the sack; the bike jarred on a stone; I shoved it frantically around the corner and out of sight before collapsing.

Ron found me an hour later only one mile from the station.

"What's going on?" He stood in the middle of the wet deserted road, laughing. I must have looked terrible in Grandad's Wellingtons, my gaberdine mud-streaked, coal dust doubtlessly streaking my face. I told him what was going on.

"Everyone's against us," I panted, fighting the sack which was again lopsidedly urging my bike to lie down. "Mum sends me or Mavis to the village for the rations and she sees no one. No one at all."

Ron looked uncomfortable.

"Come on. Let me have a turn." He heaved at the foolish deadweight and got it upright and leaning against the saddle. Easily he pushed the bike up the hill. I noticed how tall he had become. And his face wasn't round anymore, it was long and thin. He said, "Letter from my dad this morning. He's been made a Leading Aircraftsman."

I remembered Mr. Morgan as from another life, ambling along the lanes all summer long, clearing the ditches, thrashing back the nettles. He deserved promotion.

"Course he's still a batman. He wanted to service the aircraft as they came in but he never got the hang of engines." Ron smiled lovingly and then remembered to ask, "Any news of your dad?"

"Not since Christmas. He doesn't say much. Only that he hopes they've got plenty of beer at the Plume. He doesn't know about Grandad yet. It's funny really. Dad doesn't know so he can't miss him. I'm at school all week — or Aunt Flo's — so I don't miss Grandad all that much. It's Mum who

118

misses him — and they used to be always fighting."
I swallowed and then burst out suddenly, "I hate everyone here. Even Nan. They're so narrow-minded and they think they're the whole world —"

"Well they are in a way. The world's made up of people like them."

"No!"

"Yes. How d'you think the Nazis got started? Little groups of people can be spiteful just as they can be kind and good."

"You mean — the villagers are the same as the Nazis?"

"I mean people — together — including me and you, Lil — can be swayed. Do stupid things."

I thought about it, then I said definitely, "Not Phil."

His smile was as sweet as ever. "No. Not Phil."

We walked slowly on for a while, bound by our agreement. He paused for a rest, the coal tipped against his long trousered leg.

"Lil —" He took some deep breaths of the heavy wet air. "I called for you just now. I wanted to tell you something and I never see you these days."

A little spurt of happiness started in me. I laughed. "Four days each week we go to school together — haven't you noticed me sitting next to you?"

"Privately. You know what I mean."

I took the bike off him and hung on to it while he flexed his arms. The rain, iron cold as February rain can be, numbed our faces and soaked into our school gaberdines inexorably.

"I have to tell someone, Lil. You're the only one who will understand."

He was half a head taller than me. Looking at his long profile, I saw him quite suddenly as a man. There had always been something stable and mature about Ron even as a five-year-old. He would be grown up long before any of us.

He said softly, "I love someone, Lil. It's the most wonderful feeling. It's with me all the time . . . I've loved before of course. People, animals, especially animals. But this is different. It's like a light. It makes everything else shine as well. Can you understand that, Lil? It makes everything light."

I stared at him, my heart beating with long, slow thuds. Dad had not known what love was at thirty-two. But I didn't doubt Ron for an instant.

I said, "You can't be certain, Ron. You might change or anything —"

He turned to me, laughing. His face was beaded with rain, wide open, completely vulnerable.

"Of course! But I know what it's like, Lil. That's what I want to tell you. Lil — it's *glorious*!"

"Glorious. Yes," I repeated in a small voice. I remembered the feeling of glory, of transcending above pain and misery and pettiness. But not for a long time. I associated glory with heroics . . . with being brave; and I knew now the full depths of my own cowardice. I did not associate it with love.

Ron said baldly, "It's Miss Crail. You guessed, I expect."

I hadn't. I should have but I hadn't.

He adjusted the sack of coal and took the bike again.

"You don't have to say anything. I know it's daft. I don't expect anything of it. I'm trying — I'm trying to simply recognize my own feelings."

We walked on in silence. There was a metallic taste in my mouth. Was I jealous of Ron in a possessive way? Or envious of his exaltation?

He wheeled the bike down the track and propped it against the kitchen wall.

"I'm glad I told you, Lil," he said with his slow smile. "I feel as if I've been carrying it around with me too tightly. Now I've put it down and I can look at it. I miss Phil," he added matter-of-factly.

And then, if that wasn't enough, he turned toward me with a sudden thought.

"The village . . . they don't like your mum seeing so much of Mr. Edwards. Perhaps you should mention it."

CHAPTER
ELEVEN

I never doubted that Mum was "carrying on" with Mr. Edwards. Perhaps I even wanted to believe it. I told Mum I was feeling very tired and could I stay with Aunt Flo all week. On one of our Sundays together it was arranged. The pattern of life changed. Mum and Mavis came to Lake Cottage at weekends. Bob was nearly always there, too, and other Americans. They brought food with them, music, laughter. We went rowing on the river and later we would listen to Bob playing Beethoven. The summer passed. I hadn't had a letter from Dad for eight months. In defiance of him I was on the lookout for Ron's "glory."

It came just after my fourteenth birthday.

The small Cheltenham theater was very crowded. It was a Noel Coward play, and several girls from school were there with their parents. I pointed them out to Phil just as I had three years previously at the Warden's pantomime and she smiled, not understanding anything and whispering she wanted to sing a song. Bob leaned over.

"Listen, Flippa. Let's not sing here. Let's wait until we're going home, huh?"

Philippa nodded happily and watched the rest of the play with glazed eyes. I loved every minute of it. The short slick lines of dialogue made me feel sophisticated; Mum and Aunt Flo glanced at me as they laughed, inviting me to join them; Uncle Bert whispered, "Bit near the blue-pencil bone, eh Lil?" Bob gave rueful, upside-down grins and plied Mavis with chewing gum. At the interval we walked along the gallery to stretch our legs and see what the other women were wearing. I was on a pinnacle of excitement. Something was going to happen. I knew it.

We caught the 10:20 back to Gloucester and walked from the station. It was frosty and the night was full of stars and we had the roads entirely to ourselves. We sang "Mr. Franklin D. Roosevelt Jones" and Bob and I quick-stepped. Then we sang the song from the play we'd seen — "I'll be loving you — always." It was a waltz and this time Bob danced with Mum. We were making a lot of noise and on our way past the school, doors opened and a voice said, "It's all right, it's only a load of drunks." That started off Uncle Bert. He staggered from gutter to gutter shouting, "Roll me over in the clover," and Aunt Flo hit him with her handbag and told him to behave himself "*devant les enfants.*" She couldn't have meant me as I knew more French than she did.

But somehow during all this I knew that if something was going to happen I had to make it happen, so I stooped down to fiddle with my shoe and Bob lingered with me.

"Okay, honeybun?" His hair looked luminous and frosty.

"Shoe's undone —" I pulled at the laces quickly. "I can't quite see —"

"I'll do it." He knelt before me, head downbent, fingers feeling their way to my shoe via my ankle. Quickly, surreptitiously, I touched his hair. He looked up.

"Lil?" He stared at me closely, then cupped my face. "Lil — you're crying. What's up?"

I gulped a mouthful of cold night air to avoid sniffing.

"Nothing."

"Lil —" He stood up, taking me with him. "Come on. Tell me — why are you unhappy?"

"Not unhappy." I smiled and the tears rolled down my face. "I'm happy. Very, very happy." He went on frowning and staring down at me and I had to sniff. Then I said, "I love you, Bob."

Behind his head the stars were a halo; light was shooting everywhere — from his hair, his eyes, the laurel leaves surrounding a secluded garden, even loose stones in the gutter. There is no mistaking glory when you actually see it.

He put his arms around me and held me against his shoulder. Mum's voice called back, "Lil? Come on. You'll catch your death hanging about in this weather." Bob called in return, "Just coming, Grace — just coming —" and he went on holding me very tightly against him, one hand pressing my hair against the back of my neck, the other encircling the waist of my gaberdine. I didn't move a muscle. I tried to remember everything, his arms, his coat against my cheek, the rhythmic reverberation that was his heart, the smell of frost and tweed . . . the very life that was Bob.

He said, "Listen, baby. Since last year when you told me about your father, I've thought of myself in that role. I've imagined what it would be like coming home to a daughter like you every night. I've talked as I guessed your father would talk to you — our dancing lessons, the music — your math — I — I've been happier than I've been before — ever. I mean that, Lil." His hold tightened still more. "You and Philippa — your aunt and your mother — you're my family, Lil. I love you all. Can you understand, baby? I love you. Just as your father loves you."

I moved my head up and down. I was smiling. Ron was right, it was enough to recognize this love. I didn't want anything more of it. There it was, amorphous, incandescent, beautiful. And — for whatever reason — acceptable also. Yes, it was enough. I nodded again.

"You're not unhappy, sweetheart? You're all right?" Another nod, but he wasn't satisfied. He held me away from him, peering at me again in the darkness. "You're sure, Lil? I haven't made you unhappy?"

I smiled, showing my teeth so that they would glint at him.

"How could love make anyone unhappy?" I whispered. I scrubbed at my face with the back of my knitted glove. "I'm happier than happy." I snuffled a laugh. "Thank you, Bob."

He laughed, too, relieved. Then he pulled my arm through his and we began to walk again.

"Gosh, Lil, I thought . . . I couldn't bear to hurt you, honey. You wouldn't let that happen, would you?"

"No." I matched my stride to his. "You couldn't hurt me, Bob."

"Promise?"

"Promise." I walked lightly, like a ballerina. I was completely in control of my destiny and I knew how the Noel Coward characters had felt. They told themselves what was going to happen and how they would feel. And it happened and they felt.

As we turned into the gateway of Lake Cottage Aunt Flo said, "You know, Grace, Lily's going to have style. She makes that old gaberdine look like a coat from Paris."

Mum laughed and Bob said, "She's beautiful — just beautiful." He closed the gate and added, "You're all beautiful — did you know that?"

Uncle Bert lifted Aunt Flo off the ground, making her screech aloud.

"My beautiful women. Haven't I always said that? My beautiful women."

A different doctor came to the house to see Phil. He was with her for over an hour, examining her, talking to her, writing notes. Aunt Flo and Uncle Bert walked out to his car with him and then Mum put her arms around Aunt Flo and led her to the chair by the fire as if she were the invalid.

"Rest and quiet. Fresh air. There's no physical reason for the sickness. He says she seems a happy, contented child —"

Uncle Bert blustered, "They don't know a thing, these doctors. She's always been liable to throw up, has Phil. You know that, Grace — for goodness' sake tell your sister she's fussing about nothing."

Mavis pushed a piece of paper into my hand. We were sitting by the piano — I always sat by the piano when Bob wasn't there and he hadn't appeared that weekend. I took the paper.

Mum said thoughtfully, "What about a week or two with Mavis and me? She seemed to be better in the hills. Perhaps the atmosphere down here is too smoky for her."

Uncle Bert leaned forward eagerly. "What a good idea. Grace — you could manage? The kid's no real trouble —"

Aunt Flo shook her head violently. "Phil's never been away from me for long. You know that, Bert."

Mavis dug her elbow into my ribs and looked meaningfully at the paper flattened on my knee. I started to unfold it and she knelt in front of me so that the others could not see.

127

Uncle Bert was reddening behind his ears. "Quite. Don't you think it might do her good?"

"You just want to get rid of her — don't think I don't know how you really feel!" The bitterness in Aunt Flo's voice was tinged with a vicious bite.

"Look here, Flo, fifteen years and I've never had you to myself once —"

I read what was on the paper. Startled, I looked at Mavis.

Mum was saying soothingly, "You know how happy Phil was during the eighteen months you were with us, Florrie. She'd miss you, of course, but I could take her for a walk most days and Mavis is there at four o'clock each day."

Mavis put her small mouth against my ear. "It must've fell out your mum's pocket when she was making my bed. It was on my bedroom floor."

I read it again. I felt sick.

Aunt Flo said, "Mavis. Yes. I wouldn't mind if Lily was still home every night, but as it is, Grace —"

I crumpled the note in my hand and said, "That's easy enough. I'll go home again with Miss Crail. I only came here in the first place to see Phil, didn't I?"

They all looked around at me. Uncle Bert started to grin.

"Good old Lil," he said. "Good old Lil. That's settled then, is it? Phil's going to get a dose of fresh air and I'm going to have my wife to myself for a couple of weeks."

Mum said, "Are you sure you can manage the journey all week long, darling? You know how it tired you before."

She didn't want me back. She could pack Mavis and Phil off to bed by seven o'clock but my homework took longer than that.

I said, "I'm fourteen now. I don't get tired anymore."

Even Aunt Flo laughed unwillingly at that. I said I'd go and tell Phil what was happening and I shot up the stairs and locked myself in the bathroom.

The writing was backward-sloping, childish, typical of many of the hill people. It said, "You are a hoar." Just that. The misspelling made it more shocking and starker than ever. I flushed it down the loo.

There was a kind of grim satisfaction in knowing that my return home regularly would put a stop to Mr. Edwards' visits. Until I realized that it would also end my encounters with Bob. Bleakly I stared through the bathroom nets at the static water tank that had once been a lake. How long would Phil be staying with us? There were only three weeks until we broke up for Christmas and then I was at home in any case. I wasn't going to see Bob until the spring term started in January.

My sacrifice made me feel no kinder toward Mum. No kinder at all.

Nan said, "So you're all back together again. Just like you was before except for your mam then. Eh? Just like before."

Ron had been chopping kindling for her and he came in to hear these words addressed to Phil. I hadn't realized Ron worked for Nan; I stared at him, recognizing him again as one of the few "whole" people I knew.

"It's nice, that." His small, thin-lipped smile dwelt on each one of us. "Isn't it, Phil? Nice?" She nodded. "Not missing your mum are you, Phil?"

She nodded again, sadly resigned. "I'll get better with Lily," she mouthed laboriously.

"Course you will. We can go sliding on Nan's pond at Christmas like we used to. Dennis Crake is making a toboggan in his woodwork class and he's going to be allowed to bring it home when they break up."

Even my cold heart lifted a little at that.

Nan said robustly, "You'll all be better together, that's for sure. This is your place. Don't you forget that. None of you." Nan's hat sat securely on her tiny knot of a bun and the outlines of her face were less vague. In her age she represented our childhood; ahead of us beckoned Bob . . . Miss Crail. I wondered how Ron coped with the absence of his love.

Freda whispered at my elbow, "D'you remember when we had a crush on Mr. Edwards? How things change."

I tried not to look at her sharply. "What d'you mean — us growing up and all?"

"Well . . . and finding out about him."

I was horror-struck. But of course Freda must *know*. Last spring Ron had said everyone knew . . . more or less. Yet it hadn't occurred to me that Freda — still my cohort at school — knew. And had kept silent.

"I suppose you've heard they're calling on him tonight? Supposed to be with a petition to leave the school at Christmas, but Dad heard they'd got a coward's white feather to give him as well. Mum says I got to keep away in case things get nasty."

Still I didn't look at her. Nan was displaying some new corn dollies and the others crowded around. I pressed my knuckles against the underside of the table.

"Tonight? Who exactly?"

"Not the school managers. That's the trouble; they says his beliefs don't affect his work. I think the Macklesses. And all the men from the lower end of the village. Some of them haven't even got kids at the school." Freda's breath caught in her throat suddenly. "Poor Mr. Edwards. When I think how he used to sing in the chapel choir. He hasn't even been for over a year now."

I was struck by Freda's sympathy and wondered whether it extended to Mum. Another thought occurred to me: Was she trying to warn me? Were "they" calling on Mum afterward? I couldn't ask her. I couldn't admit that I knew . . .

Nan and I avoided any direct conversation too, and it was Ron who said to me as we trailed home,

"Nan's pleased you're calling in again, Lil. She was worried about you."

"Nan never worried about anyone in her life. Not many people do." I forced myself to think of Bob, concerned in case I was hurt. I remembered — as so often I remembered — his frosty hair and his arm around my waist.

Ron was saying, "She worries a lot, as a matter of fact. She doesn't go around wringing her hands like Lady Macbeth, of course. But she gets irritable and spoils one of her dollies and her hat slips forward. You know that as well as I do, Lil — you're holding yourself back. You're not letting yourself enjoy everything like you used to."

I shrugged like the characters in Noel Coward's play. "You find things out, Ron. It'll happen to you. Then you'll hold yourself in tightly too. To protect yourself." As if changing the subject I took a deep breath of the wintry air and said, "I suppose you dread the thought of the school holidays, don't you?"

He glanced around, surprised. Ahead of us Phil and Freda swung Mavis between them and her shoe came off. "No. Why should I?"

"Well . . . you'll miss seeing Miss Crail each day. I thought —"

He actually laughed. I picked up Mavis' shoe; the leather was horribly soft and damp. Nothing changed in the hills.

"That's what I mean, Lil." He stood still, frowning, trying to work something out. "If you expect things of people . . . if you expect anything to develop . . . you'll probably be disappointed. If I hoped for a future for my love, then I would dread the school holidays — dread anything that stopped me seeing Miss Crail." He gazed out over the city and his face was very long and sad. "I knew it couldn't grow and develop. But it was beautiful as it was. And that had to be enough."

I gazed at him, almost with awe. "You worked it all out like that, Ron? Right from the beginning? So that it wouldn't make you unhappy?"

"No, of course not —" He smiled briefly at me. "It came to me gradually that it was the only way to see it. I had to accept what came to me and never ask for more — revel in what I had. Like Phil."

"Phil . . ." I glanced at my cousin. Still giraffelike. Bereft of her mother and sad about it. But not pining. I couldn't be like that. I still wanted to see Bob. I still blamed Mum because I couldn't see him.

We walked on. I swung Mavis' shoe and felt strangely timid of Ron.

"You said —" I cleared my throat nervously. "Did you say that it *was* beautiful? I mean — I mean — is it over now? Is it dead?"

They were words from a Paul Henreid film and he smiled again.

"I suppose when things stop growing they do eventually die, Lil. But I still love Miss Crail." His smiled broadened into a grin. "You know the water cycle — the nitrogen cycle — all those wretched cycles in biology that prove what we've known up here for years — nothing is ever wasted? Well, that's what I'm trying to keep in mind about Miss Crail. I'm not going to waste that love. I'm not going to shut it up to protect myself in case I get hurt. It's going into everything I do. It's still shining." He took the shoe from my hand and threw it ahead to Mavis. "I'm not making sense, Lil. Take no notice."

I shook my head quickly. "Yes you are. It's just that . . . I could never be like that. I never could."

"You have to work at it. All the bloody time." He sighed sharply. "Watch Phil. It comes naturally to her."

We went to help the others force Mavis' shoe over her sticky sock. I knew about Phil, of course. Hadn't she saved my life? But then again . . . how could Phil ever know about being in love?

CHAPTER
TWELVE

Phil couldn't catch a ball in her big hands, try as she would, and Bob had made her a game that completely satisfied her wish to do so. It was just an old rubber ball pierced through and threaded on a six-yard length of string. Phil would hold one end, Mavis or me the other, and we would let the ball run its length and into our waiting hands. We were playing with it in the hall after tea when Mavis scurried out of the kitchen like a gray mouse and grabbed my cardigan sleeve.

"They've just gone past," she panted excitedly. "I bin waiting at the top of the track and Farmer Crake and Mr. Giles just gone past to call for the Macklesses down at the shop."

My heart was a cold heavy lump in my chest.

"So what?" I said. "Freda said there's some sort of petition going to Mr. Edwards tonight. That's all it is."

"There'll be a row. Mebbe a fight," Mavis said gleefully, capering about under the string. "And you know why." She ducked, although I made no move toward her. "And it serves him right, too."

I flipped the ball down the string to Phil, who grabbed at it wildly as if it could escape. "Where's Mum?" I asked casually.

"Feeding chickens. Then she's doing the brawn with that pig's head. She won't know we've gone."

Sometimes it gave me the creeps the way Mavis was ahead of me. I took the ball as it wavered toward me and flipped it back.

"Feel like a walk, Phil?" I asked.

"It's dark," she said — not objecting but reminding me.

"It'll be more exciting." I wound up the string from my end. "Come on, we'll take the ball — don't bother with your coat."

"Mum and Aunt Grace say I've got to have a coat —"

"They won't even know we're *gone*. Come *on*, Phil!"

I didn't know what I hoped to accomplish. At the back of my mind was the fear that once the men had "talked" to Mr. Edwards they would turn their attention to Mum. I didn't want to protect Mum either, just myself. It mustn't come out into the open — I couldn't bear that.

We ran up the track and hurried along the deserted road. There was a moon out and a smell of the Gloucester fog that made my heart ache for the sitting room at Lake Cottage and the piano and Bob playing "Für Elise." The trees surrounding Nan's pond made a darker blob on the night and the higher hills etched a hard wavy line against the sky.

We were six miles from civilization but we could have been a million. Like Nan said, this was my place — and I knew it was capable of anything.

We caught up with the men just before the school. They had evidently arranged to meet others from the lower end of the village here and they stood in a knot muttering, beating up their anger, passing around their bravado until they mistook it for courage. I heard Mr. Mackless say, "He ain't fit to teach our littluns —" Audrey was their youngest so he had no one at the school. Then Farmer Crake said, "He knows it, too. That's why he's gev up chapeling."

There were more mutterings and then a voice, high-pitched "— White feather's too good for the likes of 'im —" and the muttering became purposeful. The group moved off.

Mavis said happily, "They're going to punch his nose. And knock his teeth down his throat. Learn him to take no notice when I wets my knicks. Learn him to say I'm capable of better work. Learn him —"

Phil moaned in her throat and grabbed my arm.

"Take it easy, Phil," I cautioned with one of Bob's phrases. "Mr. Edwards can take care of himself." No one had mentioned Mum's name. No one had suggested that Mr. Edwards was "carrying on." It didn't make sense. But it was good. "They'll talk things over and he'll get them to see reason. We ought to get back now — Mum will miss us."

Mavis hissed, "He won't get them to see reason when it comes to your precious mum, will he, Lily? All his talking won't do no good there, will it? Like that note said, she's a —" I lunged at her and she skipped onto the grass and fell over, soaking herself in dew. Mavis was somehow always wet. I yanked her upright.

"Don't you ever repeat what was in that note. D'you hear me, Mavis Purton? Do you?" I shook her violently. "D'you hear me?"

"Yes — yes — yes —" Her teeth clicked on each sibilant. I released her distastefully. She was as slippery and as flaccid as the frog spawn she had once held in her tiny fingers. "Come on, Phil, you'll be catching cold." I looked around. The darkness did not yield up Phil. "Phil? Come on, honeybun" — another of Bob's words — "come on home now. It's all right."

From the invisible road ahead her strangled voice replied. "Lily — Lily — play ball with Phil." I tried to dilate my pupils to see through the darkness. Her voice came again, further away. "Play ball, Lily. Play ball with Phil . . ."

"My God." I stared at the lump of blackness that was Mavis. "She thinks she's going home. And she's right behind those men!" A sob came from beneath me. "Mavis — don't start crying for God's sake! We've got to get after Phil —" The lump sobbed again and then suddenly bolted off in the direction of home. I said one of Uncle Bert's words but there was no time to go after her and in any case she wasn't much in the way of reinforcements. I ran fast in the direction of Phil's voice.

The men must have heard her calling to me — must have recognized her unmistakable voice — and there was complete silence along the road except for my pounding slippers. I began to wonder whether my ears had led me in the wrong direction entirely; the school wall, crusty with moss, arose on my left; I sensed the bare branches of the horse chestnut spreading over it, then the more solid mass of the building itself. The road widened . . . a rosy glow of light came from the schoolhouse window . . . Philippa was there, outside the front door. Her eyes were flashing in her big head like those of a scared horse. In front of her, held at bay for some reason, were about a dozen men thrown into jagged relief by the light from a few shaded flashlights. One of them carried a pitchfork.

I couldn't speak and breathe at the same time and my side was an agony of stitch. I skirted the men limpingly and Phil saw me.

She laughed and jumped.

"Lily! Lily, play ball with Philippa!" She ran to me, her long legs out of control, and gave me one end of her length of string. Then she backed away, laughing inanely, looking at the men as if showing off her toy, asking them to admire it. When the string was taut, it stretched like a barrier across Mr. Edwards' front door. Phil lifted her end and the ball ran jerkily toward me. The door opened and Mr. Edwards stood there.

As far as I knew Mr. Edwards had never spoken to Phil, nor Phil to him. But through me she knew him and admired him and she turned her wide face to him with easy familiarity.

"Look! Look my ball! Look my ball, Mr. Ed-dards!"

The moment stretched itself out. His eyes flicked from the men to us and back to the men again. He wasn't surprised by them but he couldn't fit us into the scene. Maybe he had been expecting them for a long time now.

A voice from behind called hoarsely into the silence, "Send 'em away, Edwards — get rid of 'em!"

He looked to his left. At me.

"What are you doing here, Lily?" His voice was weary, achingly weary.

I giggled nervously. "I don't know. I think Phil wants to show you this —" Mechanically I flipped my end of the string and the ball soared back to her. She whooped ecstatically as she grabbed it and held it aloft.

"Phil catch! Phil catch!" She ran to Mr. Edwards and put the ball and string into his limp hand. "Mr. Ed-dards. Mr. Ed-dards do it," she demanded. Phil never demanded; it wasn't like her. She jumped, she shook his arm, she tugged him to her side of the door. Someone called, "Look here, Edwards —" and I laughed loudly and called back, "When Phil sets her mind on something it's better to go along

140

with her —" and she laughed back and lifted Mr. Edwards' arm and the ball cruised down to me.

There must be a time limit for each particular crisis; it must either boil over or simmer down; the longer the delay, the less likelihood of the boiling point being reached. Nothing could be done while Phil capered around Mr. Edwards lifting and lowering his arm as if he were a puppet. Energetically I did my part, flipping the ball back to him as fast as I could as if I were physically fighting his bewilderment and mounting impatience. But it couldn't last.

He pulled away from Phil, came over to me, and took the string away.

"Lily!" His face was cold and stern and I was back in school caught talking to Audrey Mackless. "Stop this idiocy at once! If you've anything to say — say it!"

I stared up at him — not far up; I had grown a lot in three years. In the light from the schoolhouse windows he was all shadows, his crisp sandy curls lighter by contrast. Just for an agonizing moment I could understand Mum. I pulled down a shutter in my mind. Confused and sulky, my voice spoke into the darkness.

"Nothing. Nothing to say."

Phil started to wail. Mr. Edwards said, "My God —"

Then Farmer Crake was there, separate from the others, an individual again, Dennis Crake's dad.

"Look, Edwards, don't upset the kid. There's not a bit of harm in her — if she wants to see you . . . We've brought this petition. You know what it's about. We don't want you here and that's flat." He shoved a long buff-colored envelope forward. Mr. Edwards took it. A voice called, "Clear off, Edwards — clear off — that's all we want!" Mr. Mackless shouted querulously, "Give him the feather, someone — go on, he deserves that at least!" Someone was bundled forward, held something out sheepishly, it fell to the ground.

Mr. Edwards thrust the envelope into his pocket. "I think I understand, gentlemen." He sounded brisk. "If this is a representative petition then, of course, I have no choice but to resign my post. I will study it carefully, I promise you."

Phil's wailing was low and controlled, like waves on a shore. It beat almost soothingly around us while Farmer Crake shuffled and Mr. Mackless said over and over again, triumphantly, "That showed 'n — that bloody showed 'n!" And then as if at some signal the men began to retreat. We waited, Mr. Edwards, Phil, and me. I began to shiver. The cold struck up through the cardboard soles of my slippers. I wished I had let Phil fetch her coat.

Mr. Edwards slumped suddenly and was the same height as me.

"Can't you shut her up, Lily? And come inside before you catch your death —"

Phil stopped wailing and sobbed a racking sob. "Home Lil. Home Lil. Home Lil . . ."

142

I got my arms around her. I couldn't bear the thought of the schoolhouse with its neat bachelor arrangements.

"We'd better go." He protested but we were already walking. He went into the house and caught up with us before we reached the end of the playground wall. Carefully he wrapped us both in a big blanket and walked with us as far as the track. Phil wept the whole way. It took us over half an hour, and if it hadn't been for Mr. Edwards we would have fallen down half a dozen times. There was no conversation; just the tearing breath in Phil's throat, the lurching inside the blanket, the stumbling through the night, Mr. Edwards' supporting arm and then the open back door and Mum, furious and scolding, Mavis looking sly at the living-room table, Mr. Edwards, a silent silhouette at the top of the track, Mum's angry words dying in her throat. Warmth. Safety.

The next day Phil's cold seemed to be dissolving her head away. Her speech was entirely incomprehensible, she dribbled and her nose ran, and after Mum had managed to spoon half a cup of broth into her sagging mouth, she threw up.

We changed her bed between us and took the soiled linen into the bathroom.

"You know, Lil, that child's getting worse." Mum turned on the geyser and it blew back at us. "It's nothing to do with the air. She's simply getting worse."

Our mutual concern for Phil was a blessing in a way. It made a bridge between us. Last night Mum had closed the door on Mr. Edwards and followed us into the living room, fussing anxiously. She hadn't really stopped.

"She'll get better." It had been intended as reassurance but it came out like a question. For a moment there was a flutter of panic in my voice. Mum's return reassurance was instant.

"Of course she will. I meant . . . generally. Her speech. And she's so vague. I don't think she knows what's going on around her half the time."

"No . . ." It would explain a lot. After all, how could Phil possibly have known what was happening last night and worked out such a simple and cunning solution? Yet what was it Ron had said . . . Phil did not work things out? She just knew?

Mum said briskly, watching the steam from the geyser, "We must remember to take great care of her. She's not as strong as she looks."

I knew it was the nearest she would come to a reproach for last night and I said nothing. If I'd opened my mouth it might well have been to sob childishly — It's all your fault . . . your fault. As it was, I went into my room and stared through the window and was glad it was school the next day.

CHAPTER
THIRTEEN

Christmas came. Aunt Flo and Uncle Bert stayed with us for a week. There was no snow, but the grass was slippery with frost and Uncle Bert organized a grand toboggan race from the Beacon and won on Mum's tea tray, much to Dennis Crake's annoyance. Bob didn't come with them. It had been six weeks since I had seen him — eight since we had gone to Cheltenham theater to see the Noel Coward play. I looked in the mirror to see whether I was losing weight. I should have been. I could feel my loneliness inside me gnawing away all the time.

Aunt Flo gave me a dress for Christmas. It was apricot-colored Moygashel, which was a sort of linen, with turquoise cuffs and hem — I think Aunt Flo had put them on herself because of the awful length of my legs and arms. It was the best dress I'd ever had and I wanted Bob to see it. I waited till they had put their cases into GY — I think it was their car entirely now that Grandad wasn't around — then I kissed Aunt Flo and muttered, "What did poor old Bob do at Christmas?"

Aunt Flo seemed not to hear. She kissed me back, waved for the hundredth time at Phil, who was sitting in the window, and asked me to take care of her. Then as Uncle Bert started up the engine and shouted to Mum to come and stay any time, she said, "We don't see Bob now, dear. In fact the cottage is so quiet we're thinking of moving nearer the factory and taking a couple of rooms."

"A couple of rooms?" I stared at her. "But . . . but Uncle Bert would get so lonely —"

She shrugged slightly. "Not so lonely as in Lake Cottage when it's empty, Lil. We could go to the pictures — things like that."

She opened the car door and gathered the skirt of her coat to get in. I said desperately, "Haven't you seen Bob at all since — since —"

"No dear." Her smile was too bright. "He was Uncle Bert's boss, you see. It was rather awkward to entertain him such a lot. Of course the Americans are much more free and easy than we are but even so . . ." She patted my hand more naturally. "Besides, he liked to see you two girls. Once you'd gone he dropped us!" She tried to make her smile roguish. I stood back and waved with Mum and Mavis. Could that possibly be the reason for Bob's absence from Lake Cottage? My heart thumped with hope. But then . . . he knew where we were, didn't he? Well, if he didn't, he could easily have found out.

School started again. Miss Crail, Ron, Freda, every morning and afternoon; Miss Field, secure and rocklike at school; Mum, shadowy and insubstantial at home coping somehow with Mavis,

146

watching Phil. Never any callers at home . . . probably a good thing because it meant the village was prepared to forget her part in Mr. Edwards' disgrace. But it was an odd life. I read a book about an enclosed order of nuns. It reminded me of Mum and Phil.

Mr. Edwards left. Freda said he had joined the Medical Corps because that did not clash with his views on killing and he was no coward at all and she was never going to speak to any of the Crakes again. I was grateful to Freda for making no allusions whatsoever to Mum. We grew closer. Freda told me she had always loved Mr. Edwards and she was going to write to him. I didn't tell her about Bob.

In all this routine there was no Bob. I thought up a dozen schemes for getting in touch with him. One day I actually rang the factory and asked for him in an assumed voice. Then I replaced the receiver with a crash and leaned my head against the glass of the kiosk, shaking like a leaf, my hands sweating. Day followed day. I walked on the hills with Phil at weekends and we called on Nan for bottled plums and there was no Bob. Mum was a stranger and I couldn't forgive her, yet her loneliness and isolation were a weight on my conscience. Bob could have made me forget. And there was no Bob.

At the end of February Miss Crail stayed late on three successive nights for rehearsals of the school play, and we had two hours to wait until she hurried out to her gas-bag car. Freda went to the library and did her homework — probably Ron did, too. The first night I caught the bus out to the aircraft factory, hung around outside the heavily guarded gates for ten minutes, then caught the bus back. The second night I went to the Red Cross social center in town where a lot of American soldiers sat around tables playing cards. They called to me easily in a way no British serviceman ever could. They called me "long-legs" and "blondie" — I was still mouse-brown — and plied me with chewing gum. But none of them had heard of Mr. Bob Critchley. The third night I went to Lake Cottage.

Aunt Flo was not pleased to see me. She answered the door with the same flashing nervousness in her eyes that Phil had at times.

"Oh, Lily . . . it's *you*." She didn't open the door wide and her glance went behind me down the path to the gate. "Darling, I hope you haven't come for the night. We're getting rid of the furniture bit by bit and we haven't got a spare bed." She was like Joan Crawford at bay.

I stopped myself leaning forward to kiss her.

"Er . . . no. No, I just thought — we haven't seen you since Christmas and my lift is going to be late tonight so I just thought —"

She was immediately relieved. "A flying visit? Come on in then, darling. How's Philippa? I had a letter from Grace as usual on Monday and she sounded pleased with her."

I followed her across the familiar hall. It was completely bare. The stag antlers that had been such handy coat pegs were gone, the stair carpet, hall chest . . . We went into the kitchen.

"I miss her so much, Lil. She's so unchanging. Tranquil."

I nodded eagerly. "We feel that, too. Don't worry about her, Aunt Flo. She misses you, too, but she and Mum —"

"Yes. They're very close. And Grace can give her a stable home life. She knows how her father feels, you see. Of course, he tries to cover up but she knows, Lil. She's always known." Aunt Flo stared at me, her dark dark eyes drowning. Suddenly she sat down at the kitchen table and put her head in her hands. "Never marry for love, Lily. Never." She started to cry.

I didn't know what to do. I stood behind her and touched the lovely dark hair and noticed for the first time the threads of gray in it.

"Don't say that, Aunt Flo. Don't . . ." I said awkwardly.

"Grace and me . . . both the same . . ." she sobbed. "But Albert . . . independent — strong. My Bert — he *needs* me —" She looked up pleading for understanding. "He needs me, Lily. A wife's first duty is to her husband. And Phil has got you and Grace —" She looked as if she were being torn in half. I crouched down and put my arms around her, weeping with sympathy.

"Phil's all right, Aunt Flo. You don't have to worry about her anymore. Honestly —"

We held on to each other and our sobs died down. We drew apart awkwardly. Aunt Flo fished up her sleeve and found a handkerchief and blew her nose. I sniffed.

Aunt Flo said, "You're such a mature person, Lily. I know Grace talks to you. I'm sorry though. I shouldn't have given way like that."

More tears came. "I'm glad you did. I didn't realize what it was like for you. Not really."

She said dully, "You see, Bert's got to go again. I expect your mother's told you it happens now and then. He does a deal . . . It's American nylons this time — and he gets found out and he has to . . . go. It's not easy now with ration cards and identity cards and all the rest of it. I've been selling up gradually since before Christmas, so we'll have some money. I — I'm going with him this time."

I turned and stared at the back of her head. In a way it was no surprise. It had all been there in front of me ever since Mum had said evasively that day in Gloucester railway station, "He's away just now, Lil. One of his traveling jobs." But for Aunt Flo to go with him . . . it was so right, it was so noble. I would go with Bob — anywhere.

I said hoarsely, "When?"

"Soon. The sooner the better. I'm terrified they'll catch up with him before we can get away."

"Oh, Aunt Flo —" I cast myself on her knowing how I should miss her. Aunt Flo who could adapt any old dress into the height of fashion, who always had the latest news about hairstyles and makeup.

She patted my back. "There now, darling, don't cry. We'll be back when the war's over. We'll be back. Just look after Phil. You will, won't you, Lily? Look after my Phil."

I nodded passionately against her shoulder. I would dedicate the rest of my life to Phil if need be.

As I drooped back to school though, I saw that this whole thing with Aunt Flo was the excuse I needed to get in touch with Bob. We were in genuine, concrete trouble now. Bob would want to help us — he was in a unique position to do so. And I was the ideal intermediary.

I sat in Miss Crail's car, hugging to myself the thought that I could now see Bob. They talked around me. Miss Crail said, "All right, Lily?" and I laughed as I said, "Yes. Fine thanks." Freda breathed ingratiatingly, "We're dying to see the play, aren't we, Lily?" Ron coughed out his diffidence like phlegm. "Any chance of a ticket coming my way?"

I tried not to laugh aloud again but I was laughing inside. I was going to see Bob. That was all that mattered. I was still sorry for Aunt Flo, but if it hadn't been for her I wouldn't be seeing Bob. It was like the air raids on Coventry. My fortune then had been based on someone else's misfortune.

We met in the Milk Bar in Northgate Street. He hadn't changed. His clothes were shabbier and more English but his hands, teeth, and shoulders made him unmistakably American. I seemed to swell and become very soft at the sight of him, as if

I were floating on water. He smiled. He was pleased to see me. Worried but very pleased.

"Lily. Lily-flower. It's good to see you, honey."

We sat up on the high stools smiling at the lone girl who was serving behind the bar and ignoring us. I held on to the chrome handrail, frightened I would collapse onto the floor like jelly.

"I'm so glad you could come," I whispered like Freda.

"What about school?"

"I'm skipping it till break. This is important, Bob. Honestly."

"Okay. I believe you. What do you want to drink?"

"Nothing."

"Eat?"

"Nothing. I couldn't think of anywhere else except the cathedral and I wasn't certain you weren't Roman Catholic."

He laughed loudly and the girl said, "Yes?"

"I'm Presbyterian so the cathedral's okay." He took my hand and slid off the stool. He grinned at the girl. "We've had all we wanted here," he said. "Thanks."

She made a noise of disgust like a camel and ignored the woman sitting next to us. Two people fought past us to take our stools. We went out into the rain. He drew my hand through his arm.

"You're taller, Lily," he remarked just like everyone else, then immediately made it better. "I don't think you'll grow anymore. This is how you'll be now, always."

"How can you tell?" I measured my stride to his and we went back down Northgate Street and plunged into St. John's Lane.

"I'm a mathematician, aren't I? You're perfectly proportioned. Your head goes into the rest of you seven times. Besides, I know. With my inner eye." I could tell he was smiling yet I knew he was serious. "As you are now, Lily-flower, is how I will remember you all my life."

I leaned on his arm and he supported me past the little secondhand shops and into College Green. We paused a moment to look at the mass of the tower ahead of us. He said quietly, "Is it Grace?"

It took a moment to sort that out. It was queer how Bob referred to Mum as "Grace" when he spoke to me. As if we were all equals. And anyway I'd forgotten the reason I had for seeing Bob. I was with him and that was enough.

I said, "Mum? Oh, no. At least . . ." I was terribly tempted to tell him about Mr. Edwards but I didn't. "She's lonely. Phil's with us — you know about that? So Mum is even more tired than before when she just had Mavis. But . . . she's all right."

"Yes, I know about Phil." His voice was very quiet. "I know what is happening to you all. But I have no right to do anything about it."

I glanced at him swiftly, wondering whether he was talking about Uncle Bert.

"No right?" The rain was very light, hardly more than a mist. "Aren't we still friends, Bob?"

"Of course." His arm gripped my hand against his side. "Of course, Lil. If you still want me for a friend. Has Flora told you what has happened?"

"That is why I wanted to see you." We started to walk again toward the west porch. The King's School choristers filed noisily past us for choir practice.

We went into the cloisters.

"She told me yesterday. And I thought you might be able to do something about it. Help Uncle Bert somehow. So they need not run away again."

"I see. That was all she said? That Bert was in trouble?"

"He had to be found out someday, didn't he?" I let my free hand run along the cold gray stone; it was almost dark; the fan-vaulted ceiling seemed lower than usual; spring was still a long way off. "But you know how he is, Bob. He's not *wicked*, is he?"

"No. Not wicked. He's like an irresponsible kid. He's almost innocent." He let go my hand and went over to one of the shallow stone sinks where the monks used to wash their hands. I shivered. "But you see, Lil . . . if one person is getting away with that kind of petty pilfering —"

"Black market," I said swiftly. Black market was humorous, practically legitimate; anyway it sounded better than pilfering.

"Okay, black marketing. One black marketeer, Lil, breeds others. Someone is buying the stuff he gets hold of. That makes them black marketeers, too."

"A few nylon stockings," I scoffed.

"A truckload of sugar. Parachute silk. Where does it stop? Supposing someone offered him fifty pounds for the layout of the factory —"

"He's not a traitor, Bob — you said yourself he's not wicked!"

"Not at the moment. But I'm trying to show you, honey, it snowballs. Bert drives a lot of visitors around and he's got a lot of information and a big mouth."

"Bob!" I looked over at his hunched back. It was almost as if he might be going to throw up into the monks' sink.

His shoulders shrugged. "I'm sorry, Lily-bud. I had to tell you the truth. That's how it is."

I said slowly, "I was going to ask you to smooth things over for him. But you're not going to, are you?"

He turned and faced me, supporting himself on the heels of his hands against the rim of the basin. His face was white in the glimmering afternoon light.

"You still don't get it, Lil. It's me. You're going to hate me, honey, but I'm glad to be able to tell you at last. I'm the one who has reported him. I'm sorry." He bowed his head and his blond hair was an aura, hardly part of him.

There was a long silence. I wanted to ask him why he hadn't warned Uncle Bert, given him a second chance. Then I knew that of course he had, over and over again probably. And there was only one thing to say after all. I said it.

"I could never hate you, Bob. Whatever you did I could never hate you."

Thinly the King's School choristers' voices reached us, soaring as high as the tower. I walked over and took Bob's arm. I was no longer jellylike and insubstantial. We walked back to the small door into the nave. I could feel his weight against me as the full volume of the anthem surrounded us. We went slowly down the aisle and into the cathedral precinct. Like an elderly couple, we crossed the precinct and passed the secondhand shops again. He waited with me by the bus stop. The misty rain was condensing into fog and it was very cold. Still we said nothing. I was as close to Bob as I had ever been to Mum.

The bus drew up and we stood aside for people to get out.

"Will it be okay if I come and see you next Sunday?" he asked. I nodded.

He held on to me just before I left him.

"Lily," he said urgently. "If there were any way I could undo what I've done, I would."

It was his way of saying he loved me, surely.

I sat in a seat by the window and wiped clean a small space in the glass so that I could wave to him. He stood there, his hair pearled with mist. The bus chugged beneath the railway bridge toward school. I faced front.

Somehow Bob was now mine. Because he had betrayed Uncle Bert he had given himself to me. I didn't know why and I didn't try to work it out. It had happened.

CHAPTER
FOURTEEN

We had a letter from Aunt Flo postmarked Ipswich and telling us that she and Uncle Bert had got agricultural work and a cottage. There was a lot Mum didn't read out to us. Later, when Phil was outside, she told Bob and me that Aunt Flo was doing domestic work at the farmhouse so she couldn't have Phil with her.

"It's breaking her heart," she said, not knowing she was reproaching Bob.

He got up and went and stared out of the window at the crocuses burgeoning along the track indefatigably as usual. I stood by him and he draped an arm across my shoulder.

"The choice would be different for you, Grace," he said.

It wasn't a question but I heard her poking the fire as she always did when she was considering a reply to something difficult.

Then she said quietly, "There would be no choice, Bob. There never has been."

Just for a moment his arm tightened on my shoulder and then he turned back into the room and suggested we join Phil and Mavis in the garden "digging for victory."

He came most Sundays. He brought chewing gum, tins of corned beef, nylons. He didn't look at me when he announced, "All quite legal, girls. I get them from the American P.X." He grinned. "Just for the record I'm in the American Air Force now."

We were surprised, apprehensive. "Does that mean you'll be posted away?" I asked quickly.

"No. It means I can test my devices in the field, as it were."

"You mean you go on bombing raids?" Mum held a sheer nylon to the light admiringly. It was an academic question and she hardly seemed interested in the answer.

"Yes," he said briefly.

She rolled the stocking up. "Then take care of yourself please, Mr. Critchley."

He laughed. "Colonel Critchley, ma'am. At your service."

We all whooped our delight. I saluted solemnly and Mavis and Phil fell about laughing. Mum went on putting her stockings back into their bag very carefully indeed.

At Easter Aunt Flo came for two days. Bob met her at Gloucester in a jeep. The first thing we noticed about her was that she was fatter. The Joan Crawford hollows in her cheeks had gone and she had a pair of Deanna Durbin dimples instead. The second thing was that she made her strange work clothes look stylish.

"Dresses are useless up there, darlings," she said hugging Phil to her full bosom. "I'm dishing up dinners for six land girls one minute, mucking out the pigs the next, trimming a hundred and fifty oil lamps —" She laughed with us. "Honestly, I'm a jack-of-all-trades now. I didn't know I could do it. Esme — one of the land girls — let me have her old uniform and I've stuck to it — literally — ever since." She smoothed Phil's hair, kissed her, held her long hand. "You've no idea how feminine a pair of trousers can make you feel! I predict they'll be the height of fashion quite soon."

Little Dorrit sported what she called a siren suit, but apart from that, the village considered trousers damned a woman for life.

Phil jumped up and down knocking her mother's jaw shut. "Want trousers. Want trousers," she cried.

Aunt Flo held her closer, put her hand to her cheek.

"Mummy will make you a pair," she said. "Oh Phil . . . dearest Phil . . ."

They both wept and the rest of us left them to it, me shoving Mavis ahead of me.

We walked on the hills that afternoon. Aunt Flo had traveled most of the night and was tired, but she wouldn't give in. She wanted to hear about "old Mrs. Dexter," the "cranky Crakes," the "chapel Willises," even Miss Field and Miss Crail. She held out her arms to the view of the valley floor. "You keep throwing me out in disgrace!" she cried against the late March breeze. "But I'll always come back!"

Mum laughed. "The Oxendale girls," she said, mimicking one of the old friends who had turned up at Lake Cottage. "We're like this daft little island, aren't we, Flo? We don't know when we're beaten."

They stood shoulder to shoulder, their black hair flying out like banners. Phil was within her mother's arm as usual and Mum held out a hand for me too, but I pretended I didn't notice. Bob came galloping up with Mavis on his shoulders.

"Hey — we're all on the same side. Remember, girls?" he panted.

We were laughing again — we laughed nearly all the time that weekend, but even as I laughed I knew I was outside their circle now. And, ghostlike, completing it, I imagined — of all people — Ursula Cunningforth.

The school play was a great success considering it was *Doctor Faustus*. I helped Miss Field to show people to their seats; Freda had wangled herself into the makeup department behind scenes. There was a block of chairs for the Crypt and Ron sat there. He looked different with all his peers; I'd never seen him in his mortarboard before. He sat staring raptly at the stage and I tried to imagine him chopping wood for Nan, building dams in the stream, skidding down from the Beacon on Dennis Crake's sledge. Ron continually surprised.

Bob fetched Mum, Phil, and Mavis in the jeep and was introduced to Miss Field. Her translucent eyes photographed him quickly and dwelt on Phil.

"I remember you from Lillian's first year," she said and held the long dangling hand in both of hers. "You came to watch her play tennis."

Phil's face lit up. Mr. Edwards had always avoided her, but this one — my other special teacher — remembered Phil.

"Erica Lorimer," she said nasally.

Miss Field nodded. "That's right. Lillian beat Erica and won the Cup for Kyneburgh House."

All my favorite words, and Phil never forgot my favorite words.

"Lillian Freeman of Kyneburgh House," she said delightedly.

Miss Field nodded gravely. "Quite so," she said and leaned down politely to Mavis.

In the intermission we strolled on the staff terrace. Ron joined us and said how much he was enjoying the play.

"Are you really?" Mum said incredulously.

"Of course." Ron was genuinely surprised.

Bob grinned. "You're a Philistine, Grace. You prefer Noel Coward."

Mum looked sheepish.

Phil draped herself over the balustrade. "This one best. Miss Field's play is best."

Bob's grin widened still further. "I reckon you ought to be jealous of Miss Field, Grace. First Lily and now Phil."

Mum said comfortably, "Ridiculous man. If Lily loves someone, then so do I. It's as simple as that."

Mavis was tugging at my sleeve.

"I think she's a nice teacher, too," she whispered in my ear as I bent down. But I hardly heard her. I was thinking of what Mum had said.

Miss Crail emerged from backstage afterward still in her Mephistophelean makeup to tell Ron that she was having tea with the rest of the staff so could he go home with us. Ron stammered congratulations on her acting and then stood by my side, silent and bereft, while Mum and Bob collected our things. I was overwhelmed with pity for him.

"I'm sorry, Ron," I murmured inadequately.

He focused on me, surprised. "Sorry?"

"Well . . ." I looked down at my sandals for inspiration. "You know . . . it isn't enough anymore, is it? Just seeing Miss Crail."

I thought for a moment he was going to say he didn't know what I was talking about but I should have known Ron better.

"No," he admitted at last. "No." He started to move toward the door. People were thinning out and Bob was ahead of us. He leaned across Phil to say something to Mum. Ron glanced at me and smiled with great determination. "It's got to be. It can't be anything else."

We went through the echoing cloakroom and out into the Whitsun sunshine. On the first playing field some of the smaller children were playing on top of the humped mounds of the air-raid shelters, which was expressly forbidden. The staff smiled indulgently. Mavis ran to join them.

Ron said musingly, "The thing to do is to get it outside yourself. Where you can look at it. Appreciate it. If you let it get inside, it . . . it burns. It eats away an empty hole."

I nodded. But it was different for me of course. I had my love . . . it belonged to me completely.

I said, "How can you do that — get it outside? I don't see how it's possible."

Ron laughed shortly. "I'm not sure yet. Make a picture of it? Or a poem? Anyway — look at it. I did it before so I can do it again."

Ahead of us Bob rested a hand on Mum's shoulder and pointed to the cathedral tower emerging from the clutter of buildings. Mum smiled and nodded. A girl called Sandy Denning ran by. "Your father's smashing, Lillian. You didn't tell me he was home on leave." She rolled her eyes as she went past Bob; there was no time to tell her he wasn't my father.

I said to Ron, "I don't know what you're talking about. If you want Miss Crail to love you, you could make it happen! You can make anything happen if you want it enough!"

I didn't wait for his reply. I ran up to Bob and grabbed at his gesticulating arm.

"Mavis isn't supposed to muck about on top of our air-raid shelters," I said querulously. "We'll have to get her back, Bob — come on."

All the way home in the jeep I kept talking. I hardly knew what I said. I knew Ron was looking at me curiously and that Mavis giggled out loud, which she always did when I showed off. I spoke only to Bob, telling him tales about school, about Freda and then about our picnic on the Wye with Uncle Bert. He knew I was reminding him of our secret. He lifted me over the side of the jeep when we got to the house and as I clung to him he put me down gently and murmured, "It's all right, honey. It's all right."

It was as if somehow our roles had changed yet again. It was as if he was the comforter and I were the comforted. I pulled away from him and ran into the house after Mum demanding to know what was for tea.

Mum said crossly, "For goodness' sake, Lily, calm down. If this is what Miss Field does for you, I can't think how you get through her lessons at all!"

"I thought you said you weren't jealous of her!" I flared triumphantly as if I'd scored some point.

Bob spoke from the doorway. "Look, girls. I really do have to get back now. Will I see you on Sunday?"

Mum's face lost its color. "You're flying tonight?" She turned away immediately. "Sorry. I didn't mean to ask. Yes, of course. Sunday. There should be some strawberries by then."

"It'll be all right, Grace. Don't worry."

I didn't wave good-bye with the others. What right had Mum to worry about Bob? To know that he was going on a "field trip" tonight? And how could he — how dared he — reassure her?

I went up to my room. There was a dirty envelope on my pillow. I opened it. A single sheet of paper fell out. On it was written, "Your mum is a hoar." I screwed it up in my hand and squeezed my eyes tight shut.

"Teatime, Lily!" Mum called up the stairs.

"Okay."

I sounded normal. But I was screaming inside.

CHAPTER
FIFTEEN

Bob came on Sunday. And the following Sunday. We ate strawberries and had a spell of good weather. Dad wrote me a note from Italy, and I read it briefly and tore it up. One morning we got to school and found the wall painted with the words "Open Second Front Now," referring to the Allies landing in France. There were no more anonymous letters; I asked Freda a lot of questions about such letters and whether she'd ever heard of anything like that in the village. If she'd had a clue her fair skin would have colored and she'd have gasped an embarrassed laugh. She didn't do either.

Bob was very gentle and attentive toward me. He bought me a Gramophone and a record of "Für Elise" that dropped its crystal notes into my bedroom every night. His consideration and tenderness emphasized our new positions. I fought against it desperately. I tried to have a row with him so that anger could level us. I experimented with makeup and even persuaded Mum to let me have my hair permed. It had the wrong effect entirely. His paternal smile widened. The harder I tried to grow up, the more childish I became. Bob wove himself into our family inexorably. But that wasn't quite what I wanted.

At the beginning of July it happened.

Bob was staying the weekend and on the Saturday he took us to the new swimming pool at Cheltenham. It was terrific. There were two water chutes and a fountain and a sun terrace — it was like something out of Hollywood. Phil hadn't lost the confidence she'd learned in Cornwall and she was soon dog-paddling around the small pool and trying to get Mavis to come in with her. Bob and Mum went into the big pool and were lost among the bobbing heads and flailing arms. I was on pins.

We didn't have any luck with Mavis. After a bit Phil got tired and lay on the side like a beached whale next to the picnic bags and piles of clothes and shoes. Mavis sat next to her hugging her knees and managing to look like a wet cat in spite of the fact she hadn't got into the water. I said I'd fetch Mum so we could have our tea.

There was no sign of them. I climbed down the steps at the place marked four foot six inches and swam jerkily like a coot among the experts. I passed the six-foot mark after an age and knew I was definitely out of my depth. Then suddenly Mum appeared at the top of the big chute. I waved but she couldn't see me. She was miles up. She waited nervously while two others behind her sat at the top and shot down the aluminum surface shrieking with glee. Then there was no one left. She looked down at the water and shook her head. Frantically I swam to the side and held on to the rail to pull myself up. Bob was at the bottom of the chute treading water, waving an encouraging hand. Mum was wearing a blue rubber cap. She ran her finger under the chin strap still shaking her head and laughing. Then without warning, she sat down, launched herself, lifted her hands above her head, shut her eyes, and came down like a bomb. She disappeared beneath the surface. I hauled harder on the rail; Bob had gone under too. I began to count the seconds. Then they bobbed up in the middle of the pool, Mum's blue cap, Bob's short, fair hair. His arms were around her. He held her above him. Water poured from their bodies, joining them, making them one. Then there was a flurry and a splash and he went under again while she kicked out on her back, still laughing and spluttering water.

It was nothing. I told myself that as I pulled my heavy body onto the side and ran around to where Mum was. Nothing at all.

We had tea and drove home and Phil was terribly sick.

"Did she swallow much water?" Mum dabbed at the waxy face.

"How should I know?" I didn't feel I could be bothered with one of Phil's sick turns now. It came between me and what was important.

Mum cradled Phil's head. "Too much heat and excitement, I expect. Straight to bed, young lady, when we get home. I'll bring you some arrowroot and Lil will read to you."

"I don't feel well myself," I objected.

"All right. I'll read to you then." Mum's Phil-smile died as she glanced over at me. But it was Mavis who received her anger. "If you wet that seat, Mavis, I'll murder you."

Mavis looked up at Mum. I was surprised at the hot resentment in her pale eyes.

She too went to bed when we got home — her own wish. Bob and I played chess; I lost two games in fifteen minutes flat.

"Let's go for a walk," he suggested. "If you can take it, I can't. Come on, it's a lovely evening."

He called up the stairs to Mum and she called back down.

"Don't be long then."

It was the wrong thing to say. Somehow everything she had said for a long time was the wrong thing.

We walked along the road and dropped down toward Nan's pond. The willows were out in all their green; we could see the smoke from Nan's chimney as she did her evening potatoes; below us the sun turned the Severn River red.

"D'you know, Lily, I've never met your old lady, Mrs. Dexter," Bob remarked as we skirted the pond.

"No, you haven't, have you?" Something clicked in my head. "She knows about you though."

"She does? You've told her, you mean?"

"I never tell Nan things now. She knew about you . . . oh . . . four years ago. She saw you in the tea leaves when she was telling my fortune."

His deep American laugh rang out. "A man from across the sea, huh? Yes, we have those old ladies, too."

"No, seriously, Bob. I haven't thought about it for years. But she said there was a fair man and music. You're fair and you play the piano."

Bob laughed again but I was remembering something else. Nan had foretold loneliness for me. Loneliness. There had been a taste of it when Dad left, when Grandad died, when I knew that Mum and Ursula Cunningforth had done the same thing. But I couldn't be lonely when I had Bob. Could I?

I said desperately, "Bob, I want to tell you something. I've wanted to for a long time, but I couldn't somehow. Now perhaps . . . You are — Bob, you are my friend, aren't you?"

He stopped laughing and looked at me seriously.

"I'm more than a friend, Lily. You know that. You're my family."

"Yes. Well." I stopped and stared down at the stew of Gloucester after a hot day. "Well. It's Mum." I breathed a couple of times. "I don't know how to say it." I turned again to get my back properly toward him. "She started . . . she started to have me . . . before she married Dad."

"A-a-a-h . . ." Bob's sigh was light as a feather. After it he was quiet while I counted fifteen. Then he said, "Thank you for telling me, Lily."

I waited for more. Counted to twenty-five. Nothing.

"Aren't you . . . you're not disgusted?" I blurted.

171

"Disgusted? Of course I'm not, Lily-flower." He drew a quick breath. "Did you think there was some kind of shame on you, honey?" His arms came around me, his chin went on top of my head. "Lily . . . Lily . . ." I was tight against his chest; his head dropped and he kissed my ear. "Listen, baby. Don't you see how this explains such a lot? Your mother always put you first. If it hadn't been for you, Grace wouldn't have married your father. You are everything to her. There is no shame in that, is there?"

It wasn't what I'd meant. I couldn't stop now. My voice was frantic.

"There's something else. She went with Mr. Edwards. The schoolteacher. It was after Grandad died and there was only Mavis here. There were anonymous letters. It was horrible." I hiccuped. "They went to see him and drove him out. He had to leave. Mr. Edwards."

I started to cry hysterically, deliberately. Bob turned me in his arms and put my head down on his chest and stroked my hair. I thought it was all right then. I calmed down . . . I thought it was all right. I had made it happen again. Just like I'd told Ron I could make it happen.

We went on walking and he kept his arm around me, protecting and supporting me. We said nothing. It was almost like before in Gloucester in the rain. Almost. We went slowly and now and then I sniffed. We followed the stream until we were past our

172

house, then we began to climb up toward the road again. We reached it, panting and out of breath.

"All right now, Lily-bud?" Bob held his side with one hand. "We'd better keep going, otherwise Grace will worry."

Alarm tensed inside me. I tried to dawdle but he urged me along. At the track he stopped for a moment.

"I'm glad you told me . . . what you did, Lily." Bob looked over my head. "I understand now. About your mother's loneliness."

We went inside. Mum and Mavis were laying the table with bread and pickles and cheese. The living room was filled with golden light so that even Mavis looked cherubic.

Mum smiled and her teeth gleamed.

"Phil is sleeping and Mavis decided she was hungry. How about you two?"

"Hungry as hunters." Unconsciously Bob imitated Uncle Bert, pulling out our chairs, pouring lemonade with a napkin over one arm. Mavis laughed. Bob's happiness warmed us all. He was always happy, professionally happy in a way. This was different. Tonight a lid had been taken off something he usually kept shut tight. He effervesced.

It was still light at eleven o'clock because of Double Summer Time. I tried to read but the moths came through the open window and whirred around my shaded light, and I was afraid the curtains would blow and break the blackout. I put my book down and got out of bed and hung out of the window, my body aching as if I'd run miles. The light farther along in Mum's room went out. Then I heard Bob come upstairs. I jumped into bed and lay rigid with the sheet up to my chin. He should have gone down the landing to Grandad's room. He didn't. He went straight to Mum's door. Opened it. Went inside. Closed it.

For a long time I lay there, unmoving. My legs shook with the effort of bracing themselves against the foot of the bed. My eyes, open wide, burned into the dimness of the room. I forced my imagination shut, but unbidden would come explosive pictures of Mum and Bob . . . Mum and Bob.

The silence was unbroken for what seemed hours. Then there was a creak from a loose board and the bathroom door closed. Tremblingly I relaxed and at last resorted to the consolation of masturbation.

Hot tears poured down my face. I felt as I had felt when I hit Mavis and she had suddenly started to read for me. I had got what I wanted only to find it was nothing. The ultimate defeat.

CHAPTER
SIXTEEN

Freda asked, "What are you doing when we break up, Lil? Miss Field's got a camping trip going to Snowdon for ten days. Shall we put our names down?"

I knew all about the trip. I said dully, "I can't. I can't leave Mum."

"It's only ten *days*. And there's Philippa and Mavis —"

"Exactly."

"But Lil — Miss *Field*." Freda wheezed persuasion. "Anyway, that Yank goes to your place every weekend. Mrs. Mackless says —"

I grabbed her arm so she yelped. "What did Mrs. bloody Mackless say — come on — what did she say?"

"Lil, you're *hurt*ing! That's all she said. I only meant that someone would be going in to help out if you came with us."

"Are you sure that's all she said?" I shook her arm fiercely. "If she starts her filthy gossip about Bob Critchley I'll kill her. He's sorry for Phil and me because we haven't got our fathers and he takes us out. That's all."

"So you're always telling me." Freda rubbed her arm sulkily. "Anyone would think you *liked* him or something."

"You don't know what you're talking about," I told her curtly.

As far as I was concerned everyone spoke a different language now. When I was about seven I had a ruptured appendix and through the agony of it I could hear people saying, "Tell me where it hurts, dear," and "Don't worry, you'll soon be all right." I had replied to them automatically, yet I had been quite alone with my pain; no one had been able to get through that barrier, that awful preoccupation. It was the same now. Worse, because then the physical presence of Mum had been something. Now her face, her black hair, her hands and shapely legs, made me want to scream. Yet I had to be near her. I had to watch her.

Bank holiday came, and with it our seven glorious weeks of freedom. I didn't know what to do, where to be. Phil and Mavis played as usual in the stream or the air-raid shelter; I hadn't the patience for them anymore. Ron was working on the Crakes' farm with Dennis. Freda had wangled Audrey into Miss Field's trip. I spent hours lying on my bed, my mind going around and around wondering what I could do about Bob and Mum. At last I went to Nan.

176

The smell in the cottage was no longer wholesome.

"Lily, isn't it?" Nan peered out from under her hat as my silhouette blocked the doorway. "Where's Phil, then? Where's my lovely Phil?"

I hadn't been there on my own since the awful night after Grandad was buried.

"I'm on my own, Nan. She isn't very well today."

Nan sat back against her cushion.

"No. Not well. Not long for this world, Lily. Not long. Come and sit down where I can see you, girl. You're getting that tall —"

"I haven't grown since Christmas," I said quickly. "And what do you mean about Phil? Have you been looking at the leaves again?"

"No. Not the leaves, Lily. I look at Philippa. My eyes are dim but not so dim that I cannot see what's in front of them."

"She's always been like that. It doesn't mean anything. She can't get very fat when she's being sick." I hadn't come here to discuss Phil. I asked brusquely, "D'you ever read the leaves now, Nan — like you used to?"

"Sometimes. Not for you, Lily. Once is enough for everyone."

"Yes. But I wondered . . . could you read Mum's future?"

Beneath the hat the gypsy eyes gleamed for an instant with surprise.

"Your mam, Lily? Your mam's got no time for looking into the future till it comes. You know that."

177

"*I* want to know, Nan. Me. Could you tell me about Mum's future?"

"Only that 'tis close to yours, child."

I shook my head impatiently. "Of course, but —" I took a deep breath. I wasn't going to get anywhere with Nan's vague epigrams. I said harshly, "Is she going to divorce Dad? Is she going to marry someone else?"

"No."

The monosyllable was so unexpected it shocked me into momentary silence. Then I repeated it incredulously.

"*No?* Are you sure?"

"I'm never sure, Lily. One thing I can tell you about your mum. There's trouble ahead. One way or another."

I hardly heard. She wasn't going to marry Bob. She wasn't. She wasn't.

Nan's eyes watched like a tortoise's.

At last she said, "They've always been jealous of her, Lily. She was beautiful and fine and different. They'll pounce if they can."

I came back to the present, the dead fire, the smell of mouse and urine.

"Who will?"

Nan jerked her head. "Them. At the village. The Mackless woman. Crake. Even little Freda's mam, p'r'aps." The claw fingers came toward me. "She'll need you, Lily. She'll need you."

I got up quickly. "No. Not me." I swallowed. I didn't want to give away too much to Nan and I knew all I needed to know. "It — it won't come to anything. They've always disapproved of Mum but it won't come to anything." I looked around. "I'll get you some wood, shall I? And put some potatoes in the ash box?"

"Aye. Do that, girl. I forget. All the time I forget. You do that for Nan before you go."

I did it carefully and noticed that there were no jars of bottled fruit on the shelf. Of course it was summer-time and plenty of fresh stuff around, but I'd never seen the shelf empty before. If Mum wasn't going to marry Bob I could relax my vigil a bit. When Freda came home maybe we could clean up the cottage and do some cooking for Nan.

But Freda wasn't interested.

"Later, Lil. Perhaps. I'm going to stay at the Crakes' place with Audrey. There's eight bedrooms in the farmhouse — I can choose my own!"

"What about Ron?" I asked, bewildered by Freda's sudden desertion. "He used to help Nan."

Freda sniggered. "Building Miss Crail an arbor."

"An *arbor*?"

"Yes." She struck an attitude and began to quote. "'Build me a willow cabin at her gate and halloo her name to the reverberate hills — '"

"Shut up!"

"I was only saying some Shakespeare."

"I heard what you were saying. I expect Miss Crail is paying him."

Freda snorted a giggle. "How? That is the question."

"Shut up!" I repeated.

Freda flushed. "I'm getting tired of you bossing me around, Lily Freeman. You want to watch it."

"What do you mean by that?"

"What I say. You Freemans think you can get away with anything."

I flushed too and thrust my face close to Freda's. "What do you mean?" I repeated, slowly and with menace.

Freda wriggled her shoulders uncomfortably. "There's another book besides Shakespeare, you know!"

I frowned at such a meaningless comeback.

Freda saw she'd have to be a bit more explicit. "What about the skimmity ride, then?" she fired as a parting shot and went quickly into the post office.

I stayed where I was, still frowning, while the light dawned. Freda knew my favorite author was Thomas Hardy, and it was in *The Mayor of Casterbridge* that the local "scarlet woman" was given a skimmity ride. Her effigy was burned publicly. It was the ultimate disgrace.

I turned and looked through the post office window. Freda kept her back to me. If she'd looked around and breathed one of her giggles I wouldn't have taken her seriously. But she didn't.

That afternoon Bob sent the jeep up to collect Mum to take her into Gloucester to do some shopping. I watched Phil and Mavis settle down to one of their interminable games of house and slipped up to Mum's room. Almost immediately I found two notes beneath her handkerchiefs. It was where she kept old birthday cards and pretty wrapping paper. They both said quite simply, "You are a hoar." I smoothed them and put them back. I looked at the big double bed and felt sick. Skimmity ride . . . skimmity ride . . . the words had a curiously satisfying rhythm like Lillian Freeman of Kyneburgh House.

I gripped the bed rail and shook myself back to reality. But still I couldn't seem to care. If the village gave Mum a skimmity ride, well, she'd asked for it, hadn't she?

She came back at six, very quiet and white. She'd queued for cakes and I'd made tomato sandwiches. We ate in silence. No one asked her how she'd got on. I looked at my plate or through the window. It was quite by chance that I noticed she was holding Phil's hand. Illogically I was fiercely, spurtingly jealous.

We washed the dishes and Mum went straight into the bedtime routine. And then she asked me if I'd like to go for a walk.

"No thanks," I said briefly without excuse.

"I could do with some fresh air after Gloucester." Mum forced brightness into her voice. "How on earth Flo and I used to live down there all the time —"

"You go. I'll stay with Phil and Mavis."

"Mavis is asleep. Phil doesn't mind if we go. I mentioned it."

"I'd prefer to stay in," I said stiffly.

"I'd like you to come out with me." Mum opened the kitchen door wide. "Come on, Lil. Please."

She was going to tell me about Dad, of course. First, that he wasn't coming back. Next that she was divorcing him. Third that she and Bob were getting married. I might have guessed Nan would be completely wrong.

We walked up the track, then straight across the road and up the steep slippery grass that led to our particular hilltop. I tried to lag sulkily behind but it is difficult when you're scrambling upward, often on hands and knees. Eventually we came to the place where Uncle Bert had started the toboggan races last Christmas. Panting, we stood and stared downward.

"Lick your finger and draw a cross on your toes," Mum gasped, trying to make me laugh reminiscently.

Without a smile I obeyed her; keeping my knees straight, I traced a cross in spit on my dusty sandals. It had never helped the stitch pain in my side as a child. It didn't help now.

Mum said abruptly, unable to parry my mood any more, "Lil. I want to talk to you about Dad. And me."

I was like a stone wall. "I know about Dad and you. He's not coming home. I suppose you'll divorce him."

There was a long silence. I could hear Mum breathing hard still.

At last — "It wasn't that, Lil. Certainly the last letter I had from Dad told me . . . in a way . . . that he wouldn't come back. Possibly he won't. That remains to be seen. It wasn't that."

I said angrily, "Was it that you and Dad had to get married, then? So that I wouldn't be a bastard?"

"Lil!" It was a gasp. "Oh, God. Lil. How long have you known?"

"Ages."

"This bloody place . . . bloody people . . ." Mum sobbed.

"It wasn't them. It wasn't Nan. Or Freda. Or Mrs. Crake." I began to move away from her back down the hill. "Forget it!" Bob's American phrase was just right with its touch of scorn. "Just forget it!"

"No — Lil — come back. There's more, Lil. You have to know something else — you have to help me, Lil. Please come back."

She sounded like Freda with a bad asthma attack. I sat down on the grass, my back to her. The sun was setting on Gloucester making it blood red. It was about nine-thirty.

She blew her nose, took another sawing breath. I could imagine her standing behind me. I loved her. I hated her.

She spoke in a low voice. "Our parents . . . your grandparents, Lil . . . we don't speak of them, do we? Flo and me. We never mention them." She used her handkerchief again. "When Flo met your Uncle Bert and — and —"

"Got pregnant," I said, hard as iron.

"Oh, God, Lil . . . please . . ." I didn't turn. "You — you sound like my mother, Lil. Unforgiving. You *know* Aunt Flo. You love her."

I kept silent and Mum struggled audibly with herself for some time. Then she started again and now her voice was controlled.

"Father died. A heart attack while he was at work. Mother said Flo had killed him. When the same thing happened to me, she nearly went out of her mind. It was the disgrace, you see. People talking. That's why I've never tried to be friendly up here — people can hurt if you let them close to you. Anyway . . . Flo and Bert . . . they offered me a home in London. No one would have known. I liked city life — the country frightened me. But . . . Albert said he loved me. For myself. Not just because of you." A short sigh. "I chose to believe him, Lil. And as you know . . . it wasn't quite like that."

A little worm of sympathy wriggled inside me. Just for a moment. I bent my head and looked through my supporting arm at her shoes. She had small slim feet. After four years of war her shoes were still smart.

She went bleakly on.

"Mother died when you were six months old. She hadn't had anything to do with me since my wedding and she left a wish in her will that neither

Flo nor I should go to the funeral. Luckily the solicitor did not tell us until afterward. Funny really. Flo killed Father and I killed Mother."

"Don't be potty!" I cried sharply.

"Sorry. A bit melodramatic . . . sorry."

I looked back down on the city and it was blurred.

Mum said, "Lil dear, what I have to say is difficult. I've told you what happened in the past so that you will understand that it must not happen again. I should not have married Dad, my dear. I should have tried to be independent — it wasn't fair to *use* Dad in the way I did. Can you see that?"

I shook my head dumbly. She waited but I couldn't speak. She took my gesture as agreement.

"Lil, listen. I've been weak and foolish — lonely — that's what I was. Lonely. I —" Here came a huge gulping sound. "I fell in love with Bob. I couldn't help it. We were both lonely. Frightened too. He told me —"

I screamed. A single shriek that split the evening air in two.

Then I gabbled, "Don't tell me — don't tell me — don't tell me —"

"I've got to tell you!" Her voice climbed above mine. It was stern and angry. I hadn't heard it like that since I was a child. I put my hands over my ears and gripped my knees with my elbows. Her voice reached me inexorably.

"I've got to tell you, Lil, because you're the only one who can help. I've told him today to keep away.

We don't want to see him anymore. Do you understand? He mustn't come here anymore. Lil — if he gets in touch with you, you are to tell him the same thing. You've got to promise me, Lil —"

I looked around at her then in astonishment. Her face was streaked and blotched with tears as I knew mine was; her eyes, coal black and demanding, met mine.

"Why-y-y?" The word came with a sob, was elongated ridiculously.

Her lips barely moved. "I thought you would realize. I'm having a baby, Lil. It's happened again. And I can't use Bob. He mustn't know."

I don't remember pushing myself off down the hill, slithering and bumping over the molehills, standing, running, falling, at last crossing the road and making for the willows by the stream. I wanted to kill myself. I lay in the water like Ophelia but I couldn't drown. Life forced itself into me, hatefully, persistently. Wet and bedraggled, I went home when it was quite dark. Mum was waiting in the kitchen. She held out her arms to me and I brushed past her and went to my room. There was no lock on the door but I wedged a chair under the handle, and when she whispered, "Please, Lil . . ." I put the pillow over my wet hair.

The next day at teatime the jeep arrived. The American officer in it saluted when Mum opened the door to him. He had a letter for her from Bob. He told us "with great regret" that Colonel

Critchley had been killed in a bombing raid on Hamburg the previous night.

Mum stayed where she was after he'd gone and rested her head against the closed door. Phil rocked and wailed loudly. Mavis cried and knuckled her eyes. I stared at Mum's back.

Bob was gone. And I couldn't even grieve for him because of what Mum had told me.

CHAPTER
SEVENTEEN

Miss Field said calmly, "You realize yourself, Lillian, that this state of affairs cannot continue. You have started your Certificate course, and to fail consistently to produce homework —"

"A page of translation — I'll let you have it this afternoon," I said, trying to balance scorn, defiance and politeness equally.

Miss Field sighed. "It isn't only German, my dear. Now that I am your form mistress, I have complaints from other members of staff. You owe Miss Sibley no less than four English essays. Your favorite subject."

I looked at my feet and tried not to fidget.

She got up and went to one of the dormer windows.

"Lillian. I make a point of never intruding into the private lives of my girls. May I break that rule now?"

I muttered something.

"Very well. Then I will admit to you that Miss Crail has told me you are living through a very difficult time at home. The people in your village are inclined to be narrow-minded and intolerant —"

"My mother's pregnant!" I blurted angrily. "And my father's been away for three years. Not surprising they're intolerant, really, is it?"

There was a judicial silence. Then Miss Field said very quietly, "You are of their opinion?"

"She — she's no better than Ursula Cunningforth!"

"Ursula. Yes." Miss Field came back to her desk and began to put books into her rubbed leather bag. "I visit Ursula occasionally, as you probably know. She is training to be a children's nurse." I looked up, astonished. "So that she can have Mark with her when she works. Mark is her baby."

"I thought — I thought she would have him adopted. Miss Crail said —"

"Ursula wouldn't do that, Lillian." Miss Field sounded shocked. "She had the support of her parents — there was no need." She closed her bag with a decisive snap. "Is that what you want your mother to do, Lillian? Have her baby adopted?"

"I don't know . . . I hadn't thought . . ."

"Then I suggest you do. Constructive thinking should take the place of your resentment, my dear. After all, the new baby will be partly your responsibility."

Anger spurted from me. "How do you make that out?" I didn't care about being polite anymore. "I had nothing to do with it. You just don't understand —"

"You will share the same mother, Lillian. Whether you like it or not." Suddenly the tranquil gray eyes filled with pity. She leaned over the desk. "Child . . .

try to put yourself in your mother's position. She's an intelligent woman. She knew what she was doing. Yet she loved someone so much —"

I stood up. "I can't listen," I gasped. "It's horrible — horrible —"

She waited. I sat down.

"I'm sorry. I can't bear it. Honestly — you don't understand."

She spoke levelly. "When I was young in Heidelberg I loved a married man. A Graf — a count — with a position, estates . . . he couldn't give them up for me. Yet he loved me too. And even then I was fat and tongue-tied and unattractive." I looked up to protest but she couldn't see me. "He wanted me to have a holiday with him. I was frightened. Frightened of the gossip and the possible consequences." She picked up her bag. "I came home and I have not loved anyone since and I have no memories." She went to the door. "If you propose to do that translation during this dinner hour, Lillian, you had better get started. And I will try to hold the other mistresses in patient abeyance until you are able to think constructively. That is all I can do for you, my dear."

She opened the door and went out.

"Thank you, Miss Field," I said to the empty room.

That saying "to understand all is to forgive all" is a load of rubbish. I understood Mum. I understood her as if I were inside her skin. But I could not forgive her. I couldn't forgive her for anything. Mr. Edwards, Bob, even my own begetting. I didn't think I could live with her much longer. If only Aunt Flo had been nearer I would have gone to her. Halfheartedly I scanned the thin wartime papers for jobs in London. I could have lied about my age and tried to get into the armed services, but I didn't have the energy, the willpower. I muddled through the autumn and the winter waiting for something and I didn't know what. Then one night Ron stayed in Miss Crail's car when she stopped at his turning and said he'd drop off with me and go and see Nan.

"She's not too good, Lil," he said as we watched the balloon-crested Austin round the bend toward the next village. "She can't seem to eat anything anymore and she babbles on about danger all the time." I didn't say anything. He went on, "The danger is something to do with you." He hoisted his satchel more comfortably onto one shoulder. "She knows more than you realize —"

"Yes, I know," I said impatiently. "What between reading the leaves and people's eyes and collecting all the bits of gossip from the kids for miles around — there's not much escapes our Nan!"

"Listen, Lil —" He couldn't keep still for embarrassment. "I know you and Freda aren't speaking and it must be tough for you — this business —"

"Why don't you say it right out? Why don't you say —"

"Lil, shut up a minute. You make it worse for yourself by being so angry. You made Freda cry —"

"I made *Freda* cry?"

"She only wanted to warn you — like I'm trying to warn you now. Nan isn't such an old fool. You remember that fuss about Mr. Edwards —"

"Don't remind me!"

"They like stirring things up — that's all it is. They can't get away from the land and fight and they get frustrated and . . ." He let his satchel fall to the gravel with a thump. It was bulging with work. Mine was empty. He kicked at it absently. "I reckon — Nan reckons — after Christmas something might boil up."

"A skimmity ride?" I asked scornfully.

He shrugged. "I don't know. Whatever it is it could upset your mother badly and in her condition —"

"In her condition — in her condition —" I mimicked furiously. "Perhaps that would be a good thing. Perhaps she'll lose the brat then, and we can all go back to being exactly what we were before —"

He interrupted me firmly. "Is your aunty coming for Christmas, Lil?"

"I don't know."

"Why don't you write and ask her? When she sees how things are, she might stay on. Until after."

"Oh shut up."

"Lil —"

"Why don't you shut up and mind your own business, Ron Morgan? You don't know what you're talking about half the time. How's the wonderful shining love business going now? Written any good poems lately? Painted any good pictures?"

He looked down at the lump of his satchel. Then he hoisted it onto his shoulder again.

"Write to your aunty, Lil. I think you need her more than your mum does."

He walked off along the road.

I didn't write to Aunt Flo. She'd been down at half-term, and I knew she was saving up her time off to come to us in April when the baby was supposed to be born. I didn't want her coming down after Christmas anyway. Suddenly as I watched Ron march stoically away into the dusk that early December night, I knew what I had been waiting for. I wanted Mum to be punished. I wanted to see Mum punished.

Day followed day. I didn't know which was worse, early mornings when I had to face Mum on her knees doing the grate, or evenings when I pretended to do homework, Mavis drew, Phil sat staring into the fire, and Mum knitted unidentifiable clothes. Christmas arrived and then went. Aunt Flo sent Mum two smocks she'd "run up" and Mum wore them all the time. She said to me, "Why don't you put on that pretty orangey frock Flo gave you last year?" And I put it on, then took it off remembering that Bob never had seen it after all. I played "Für Elise" on the Gramophone very quietly, but when I opened my bedroom door Mum was going into the bathroom. I couldn't even enjoy his music privately.

And then came the dead time of the year. I waited.

On January tenth I went into Phil's bedroom for something and found Mavis draped half over Phil as she lay on her bed, showing her something and whispering. Phil was rocking jerkily from side to side, her eyes empty.

"What's going on?" I asked sharply. "Mavis, are you being nasty to Phil?"

Mavis skipped off the bed, stuffing something in her school uniform pocket. I grabbed her.

"Phil did ought to know," she gabbled, wriggling like an eel in my grasp. "She isn't as daft as everyone thinks. She did ought to know —"

"What were you showing her?" Phil began to wail. "Come on, Mavis, you might as well tell me."

"It's only God's truth." Mavis jerked convulsively and was free. "She did ought to know, Lily. Silly Lily!" She giggled and whipped through the door. As she went, she flung a snippet of paper behind her. "It was only that. Silly Lily!"

I didn't bother to pick up the paper. I knew what it was. Wearily I turned to the bed.

"Come on, Phil, cheer up. It's always darkest before the dawn and all that sort of rubbish." I sat down by her and held her, and we rocked together. It was the first comforting thing that had happened since August. I remembered my resolution to dedicate my life to Phil. It had got lost somewhere.

When she stopped making a noise I wiped her face and chafed her cold hands.

"All right now, Phil? Let's go down and have some cocoa. Then we'll have a nice walk into the village for the rations. Shall we?"

She looked past me.

"Mr. Edwards," she whispered.

"Yes. Yes. She didn't spare you much did she, our Mavis? Come on, Phil —"

"They were going to hurt Mr. Edwards."

"Not while we were there. Don't you remember?" I remembered. Phil standing there playing with the ball Bob had made her. I put my arms around her again. "Oh, Phil —"

She struggled free and looked wildly at me.

I said, "What's up? D'you feel sick?"

"No. No. No. No —"

"All *right*, Phil. Now come on. You're frozen and if you get much thinner you'll be invisible. Come on."

She came. She drank cocoa obediently and put on her thick coat and gloves and the same awful pixie hood from four years ago. Mum silently handed me the ration books and some money and we set off. There was no sign of Mavis. I promised myself I would hit her hard when I saw her next.

As usual people avoided us in the grocer's and the butcher's. It usually made no difference to Phil. She would smile and hold my hand and sniff the smells like a contented dog. Today she did not smile; she looked around her furtively, and when Mrs. Crake came through the door she did not take her eyes off her once. Mrs. Crake went to the counter nervously and began to talk to Mrs. Mackless. I heard Mrs. Mackless discussing a family who had nothing to keep them in the village and ought to leave very soon. With a shock I realized she meant us. I hurried Phil outside.

On the way home Phil suddenly said she wanted to see Nan.

"Not now." I was tired, yet oddly excited. "Not now, Phil. Tomorrow maybe."

"I go by myself," she announced stubbornly, letting go my hand. "Want to see Nan. Now."

She often went by herself so I didn't protest too much. I stood on the edge of the track and watched her lollop over the fields. The air was cold enough to hurt my chest. She looked like the stick men we used to draw. I resolved to stay close to her in the future.

There was the sound of a horse and trap behind me, and I began to hurry out of sight of the road. Then Mrs. Willis called me in her high voice.

"Lily, is that you? Wait a minute, there's a love —"

I waited and her fat pony high-stepped behind me.

"Lily — I'm glad to see you. I was coming for a word with your mother but it's so awkward . . . so awkward . . ."

Unwillingly I went to the trap. Mrs. Willis was flushed and very breathless as if she'd run here instead of driving.

She said, "Lily — Freda's told me how you hate to talk about . . . my dear, it's so awful for you. Not your fault after all — poor innocent child. We understand. Freda and me. We understand, Lily."

I held the edge of the trap and waited. Something stopped me running off. I waited.

"I heard just this morning, Lily. Audrey told Freda and Freda ran as fast as she could . . . you know she stays at the Crake farm with Audrey every weekend. It makes a change for her, you see, dear. We're so cramped in our little cottage, and Freda doesn't get on with our evacuee like you do with yours. Anyway, dear, the Crakes and Macklesses and — oh, I don't know who else — they've signed a petition asking your poor mother to leave the village."

"A petition?" The words were yanked out of me. "Is that all?"

"Well, dear, I don't know about 'all.' It's not very nice, is it, to have your neighbors get together and ask you to get out of your home. Harsh words will be said, Lily — make no mistake about that. It won't do your mother much good, will it?"

"No. No, I suppose not." My mind clicked over coldly. "Have you any idea when they're coming?"

"This afternoon, dear. And I think if you and Philippa answer the door — just take the petition — don't let your mother be seen. Can you persuade her to lie down or something? Then maybe you could write to her sister and sort something out."

"Yes. Yes. Perhaps." This afternoon.

"You wouldn't realize it, dear, but when Farmer Crake called on Mr. Edwards that time — d'you remember your Philippa had run off or something and you were there? It might well have avoided a lot of unpleasantness. Somehow no one can be nasty in front of your Philippa."

And Philippa was at Nan's. How could I keep her there?

Mrs. Willis thinned her lips. "I did think I'd get a word of thanks, actually. I left my baking and rushed out to borrow the trap the minute Freda came in —"

"Yes, of course. Thank you, Mrs. Willis."

The trap turned on its own axis as the pony skipped around. Mrs. Willis sniffed.

"Now don't forget, Lily. You're the only person who can do anything about this —"

"All right. Yes. Thanks, Mrs. Willis." I couldn't wait for her to go.

She flipped the reins and the pony started forward.

"Shall I send Freda around at teatime to see how you are?"

"No. No, don't do that. Mum might be upset," I called.

I think she sniffed again.

I went to the house and found Mum ironing. There was no sign of Mavis.

Mum tried to sound bright.

"Was that Mrs. Willis I saw in the trap just then?"

"Yes."

"What did she want?"

"Nothing." I realized that was no good. "Freda," I amended. "She was looking for Freda."

"Oh." Mum ironed briskly, wondering what to say next. That's how it was now. She came up with — "Dinner's all ready. Where's Phil?"

"Gone to Nan's. I'll dish up and put hers on top of a saucepan, shall I?" I pushed past Mum, anxious to get dinner over. Mum was surprised. I rarely offered to help her now.

Mavis appeared as if by magic at the rattle of the plates. She sat on the other side of the table eyeing me nervously. I recalled I had wanted to hit her for something but couldn't remember what. Immediately after she'd bolted the last of her pudding, she whispered something inaudible and went upstairs. Mum called after her, "Mavis, get another cardigan if you're staying up there; it's so cold." It was cold. As I shook the tablecloth, a few flakes of snow blew into my face.

Mum said, "Where's Phil got to? She shouldn't be out in weather like this. If she isn't back in the next ten minutes, I'm going after her."

Mum had to stay in. My mind was hot and muddled but I knew she had to stay in.

"I'll go and look for her. She's probably having a baked potato with Nan and forgot the time."

"Nan never forgets the time. She always sends you children home for meals." Mum took the kettle off the stove and poured hot water onto our dishes. Her stomach preceded her whatever she did. I shuddered.

She went on almost to herself. "I'm going to write to that doctor who saw Phil last year at Lake Cottage. He might agree to come up here and have a look at her . . . in the circumstances."

"She's all *right*. Don't worry so."

"Of course she's not all right —" Mum forgot herself and really snapped at me. "She's not eighty-four pounds and she's taller than you. There must be something they can do." She peered through the steamy window as she pushed the dishes about. "Where the dickens *is* the child? Surely she knows her way home by now?"

I threw down the teacloth. "I'll go down to Nan's." I pushed my feet into Grandad's Wellingtons — they were a good fit now — and reached my school gaberdine from the hook on the door. The clock on the mantelpiece stood at quarter past two. I registered that.

I went up the track onto the road. The snow came in small flurries — nothing to worry about — but it was desperately cold. I cut down over the fields immediately and slithered on the frosty grass parallel with our track until I came to the Cotswold-stone wall that divided our vegetables and chickens and air-raid shelter from the rest of the hills. I crouched and ran alongside it until I was level with the door. Through the crenellations at the top, I could watch the house. Across the fields on my other side I should spot Phil as she came from Nan's. I huddled down to wait.

Dad used to mock some of the village elders with a favorite saying of his, "Sometimes I sits and thinks and sometimes I just sits." I must have just sat out that afternoon. I was conscious of the cold; I knew when Mum came out at regular intervals with her old mack clutched around her and looked wildly over the top of my head and then went inside. I heard her call Mavis all over the house and then down the garden. Mavis must have slipped out before I had. I knew too that the snow was thicker and that it was getting dark. Otherwise I didn't think. I was waiting.

Eventually they came. I didn't see them arrive; I couldn't see the track or the road from my hiding place, but suddenly they were there. About six of them. Only two men — strangers to me — and four women. Mrs. Mackless was there. A woman who served in the shop. Mrs. Crake all done up in scarves as if ashamed to be recognized. A Mrs. Thompson who cleaned the vicarage for Little Dorrit.

I straightened slightly, my limbs in pain. Mrs. Mackless hammered on the door, not gently. It opened with a jerk. Mum surveyed the little crowd in the light from the kitchen.

"Oh, my God — is it Lily?" She looked like a crazy woman. Her dark hair stood in spikes around her head and her hands were stretched out toward Mrs. Mackless, pleadingly. The blue smock, carefully pleated by Aunt Flo to give maximum fullness in front, was creased as if she'd been tying it in knots. "Lily — where's my Lily?" Her voice rose frantically.

Mrs. Mackless did not know what to do. She glanced at the others. Then she cleared her throat.

"We don't know about Lily, Mrs. Freeman. We've come here on another errand entirely. We don't consider you are a fit person to live —"

"Where's Lily? Where's Philippa?" Mum's voice was suddenly strong. She pulled her smock down tautly. "Where are my girls?"

"We've got this petition together, Mrs. Freeman, asking you to leave the village. There's nothing to keep you here now that old Mr. Freeman is gone and your husband not coming back —"

Mum turned from her impatiently.

"Don't you understand what I'm saying?" She searched the group and seized on Mrs. Crake. She shook her by the arm. "Philippa went to see Mrs. Dexter. She was late. Lily went to look for her — she's been gone for two hours! Look at this weather — you know how delicate Philippa is —"

Mrs. Mackless said grimly, "Just you take this petition, Grace Freeman, and read it carefully. You're nothing more than a Jezebel. A fine example for our own girls —"

Mum snatched the piece of paper and threw it from her irritably. It was caught by a flitter of wind and whisked over the wall to my feet. The ink was running already. There were about thirty names but that meant only fifteen houses, probably less. Not enough people to organize a skimmity ride. Not enough people to matter.

She snapped. "Never mind that now. It's lucky you've come. We must start a proper search —"

Someone else was running down the track. I pressed my numb face against the stone. It was Ron.

He skidded to a halt in front of Mum; between Mum and Mrs. Mackless.

"Are you okay, Mrs. Freeman? Where's Lily? I came as soon as I heard —" He choked on his breath. He wore a green sweater I remembered from years ago; it rode up over his shirt and had holes in both elbows. On his feet were ancient slippers.

Mum dropped Mrs. Crake's arm and took Ron's.

"We've got to search properly, Ron. Where would they go? Where would Phil go?" She babbled on and Ron gradually got the story. He held on to her with one hand and to his side with the other, nodding, brushing snow off his nose. The petition, the skimmity ride, it was all forgotten. It was like a game of chess when you make a diabolical move only to find you have put yourself in check. It had seemed essential to keep Phil and me out of the way, to make Mum face her "punishment" alone.

Yet it had been our absence that nullified everything.

What happened then? They all went. Chivvied by Ron, Mum went in by the fire, and Mrs. Crake went to fetch her husband and meet Ron by Nan's pond. It was dark and snowing properly. Numbly, achingly, I stood up and began to slither down to Nan's. I thought it was over. I didn't bother to think up excuses for my long absence. I would fetch Phil from Nan's and everything would be the same. My waiting had been . . . in the end . . . for nothing.

I got to Nan's well ahead of Ron. Her oil lamp made the uncurtained window bright yellow — the wardens had given up pestering her about the blackout, which showed that we were winning the war. I knocked and went straight in.

Nan was alone. She was in her chair as usual, her hat skewered to her head, her face turned toward the smouldering fire. The smell was awful.

"Where's Phil?"

My breath steamed and I radiated cold. Snow dripped off my cuffs and hem.

Nan looked up slowly, unsurprised.

"Gone. Gone, my Lily." She stared at me with difficulty. Her head dropped again. "I couldn't have stopped her if I'd tried. But I didn't try all that hard. It's maybe for the best."

"What do you mean — gone? She hasn't got back home yet. It must have been one o'clock when she arrived here." I went to the table and leaned on it.

The corn dollies Phil had made over the last year were laid in a row there.

Nan slumped a little further into her chair.

"She didn't stay long. Told me what was happening to your mam. The letters. The talk in the village. Asked me what they were going to do. I told her as much as I knew. She said she was going to run off."

"Run off?" I felt sick. Phil. Running. Alone. In the hills. I forced myself to breathe. "What did you tell her, Nan?"

"I told her some of the busybody women were going to call on your mam at teatime today and try and get her to leave."

"And she was scared. She ran away."

"You know better than that, Lily!" The old sharpness was back in Nan's voice. "That's what everyone else will say. Not you, my girl."

The blood started to move in my fingers and they pained terribly.

I protested hopelessly. "She wouldn't work it out, Nan! Laying a false trail — Phil couldn't work it out."

Nan said heavily, "All she do know is that if they're out looking for her they can't be pestering your mam."

"But this weather — she won't find her way back!" Terror and pain were inseparable. I tried to pick up one of the corn dollies, and my fingers would not work.

"I told her that, Lily. I did my best." The hat nodded toward the fire. "She kept on about Mr. Edwards. I didn't know what she meant."

I knew. If Phil had dashed to help a man she did not know, a man who could never bring himself to speak to her, how much more would she do for Mum?

When Ron burst into the cottage a few minutes later, I had managed to pick up one of the corn dollies and my hands were thawing in my own tears.

But they were too late.

CHAPTER
EIGHTEEN

That night was very long. No one would let me do anything to help look for Phil although I knew all the places she would go. I accepted my inactivity as a just punishment; I had seven hours in which to assess, examine, and take the full weight of my guilt. Strangely, it occurred to no one else that I was responsible for Phil's disappearance. In fact they all seemed eager to assume the blame themselves. Mum said nothing, but her white face and fluttering hands over her swelling smock told their own story. Mrs. Crake spent two hours leaning over our fire, keening one minute and moaning the next, "It was our fault. The child got wind of the petition from old Mrs. Dexter and was so frightened . . . so scared . . . It was all our fault." Nan repeated like an incantation, "I tried to stop her . . . I tried to stop her . . ." Only Ron, appearing every two hours in the hope that she had been found, tramped the sheep paths he knew so well free of guilt, forging ahead of the older men so that he could call through the wind with absolute truth, "It's only me, Phil — it's Ron — I'm by myself — where are you?"

It was Ron who found her at midnight. She was not far from home and had managed to wedge herself in the hole of a tree that grew from the side of the hill and made a kind of balcony we had used in many games. She would have stayed there, completely invisible from the path, if Ron hadn't remembered it and swung himself across in the driving snow. He found her huddled in an ungainly heap, her pixie hood sodden and caked with freezing snow, one shoe missing, her eyes half closed. He did not leave her. He wrapped his body around her as best he could and shouted at regular intervals until Mr. Willis heard him and the ambulance came from Stroud. He said she did not wail or even rock herself. She smiled at him as if she was glad to see him. And when she heard him calling the others, she must have known that her instinctive plan had worked and Mum was safe. But Ron did not know about that, of course. He said very simply, "She trusted me. She's always trusted me. She knows I'm her friend."

We went to Stroud the next morning although visiting was from two till four. Matron met us, her lips pursed, her blue eyes like large marbles.

"Mrs. Freeman? Yes. I understand you are the aunt and *in loco parentis*." She glanced at me. "Certainly no children are allowed."

"I've got to see her," I said stubbornly.

Mum was at her best. "Lily will come with me to see Philippa. How is she this morning, Matron?"

The eyes swiveled for a moment and then gave in.

"Not well. Children of her sort rarely live this long."

Mum gripped my arm, and I swallowed my cry of protest. "We know that. But at least she is alive. She survived a long time in that snow yesterday. Surely that is a good sign?"

"She is very emaciated, Mrs. Freeman. Has her mother been sent for?"

"Yes. She will be here this afternoon. Meanwhile we will stay with Philippa."

"She's not taking any notice of anyone." The pale gaze surveyed me again reluctantly and again capitulated against Mum's determination. "Very well. If she becomes disturbed you will have to leave, of course. This way."

I restrained Mum slightly. "You never said —" My hoarse whisper was audible to the starched figure ahead. "You never told me Phil didn't — Phil didn't —"

With a rustle Matron held open a swing door. She said professionally, "Mongoloids of that particular type rarely live far into puberty."

Mum swept me into a small three-bedded ward. "Philippa has never been diagnosed as mongoloid," she said coldly. "She has slight cerebral palsy, of course, but —"

Phil heard her voice and raised her head. She looked like a rabbit injured by a car as she turned toward us questingly. Her skull was very prominent; eyes sunken, mouth shrunk away from too-large teeth, nose pulled tightly upward showing distended nostrils.

"Grace!" she called. "Grace . . . Lily . . . Grace . . . Lily . . ."

We reached her together, our arms entwining to make a cradle for her head and shoulders. Her hair felt sharp and coarse. She rocked gently and we had to go with her. Matron watched us disapprovingly for a few seconds and then left.

Mum whispered, "There, Phil . . . there, darling. Everything's all right now. Aunty Grace and Lily are with you."

"Grace." Phil put her head over to one side so that she could look at Mum. "Grace."

I found I was crying again. More of those tears that were now so useless. As once before, Phil wrapped her arms around me and comforted me.

Aunt Flo said firmly, "No one is to blame. I could easily say it is my fault for leaving her but I'm not going to. The best thing for Phil was the freedom she could have up here. We don't know why she wanted to run off last night, but she did. She had a good reason for doing it. I wanted Phil to be free. However dangerous it was."

Mum said, "Flo, she stands a good chance. Don't talk as if — as if —"

"Darlings. Please face up to it. If Phil gets over this she won't live long." Aunt Flo rubbed the palms of her hands down her Land Army trousers. "The specialist — in Gloucester — he said it was a miracle she was still alive then. She has a rupture in her stomach wall . . . I explained this to Grace, Lily. I did not know what to do. Bert is still a young man —"

"I understand," I said quickly. I looked at Mum. I remembered her saying to Bob, "There would be no choice."

Mum said, "Let's get her home, Flo. We can keep her going on arrowroot, and after this damned war is over maybe there will be an operation —"

"Maybe." Aunt Flo studied her hands. "Bert is coming down at the end of the week. For a few days."

Mum's eyes met mine, startled. I wondered why.

Phil died the night he arrived. I'd been with her in the afternoon, and she'd said all our names slowly and clearly. "Mum . . . Dad . . . Grace . . . Lily . . . Nan . . . Ron . . . Freda . . . Mavis . . ." Then she'd smiled and said "Lillian Freeman of Kyneburgh House" as precisely as her cleft palate would allow. I couldn't believe it when they told me the next morning she'd gone. Only Uncle Bert, weeping into his hands, convinced me.

Grandad, Bob, and now Phil.

All the village was at her funeral. She took all the nastiness, all the pettiness with her. But she left a vacuum and vacuums should be filled. Ron, Dennis, Freda, and Audrey put flowers on her grave regularly and offered me some of their candy ration, but our old camaraderie was gone. Mum got offers of help but no one called at our house. We were in limbo. I played truant from school and walked the wet February hills alone, remembering Phil and Bob.

At half-term Miss Field called.

I was cleaning the windows and saw Miss Crail's car turn down the track; Miss Field called from the passenger side.

"Lillian. Miss Crail can pick me up again in half an hour. May I call on your mother for that time?"

I wanted to shrug and say, "If you like," but my high school training was four years old and too deep.

"Of course." I climbed from the kitchen chair — not long ago I would have jumped down. "Good morning, Miss Crail. Will you come in, too?"

"No thank you. I have some shopping to do in Stroud. Miss Field is staying with me for half-term." She didn't quite meet my eyes. Was my truancy so disgraceful, or was it Mum?

Miss Field was as always, courteous, friendly, rocklike. She asked Mum how she was, greeted Mavis by name, and then said with deep sincerity, "I want to tell you how sorry I am that Philippa is dead."

It was the first time anyone had mentioned Phil's death directly. The villagers had said she was "gone."

Mum smiled slightly. "Thank you. It is kind of you to come. Had you met Philippa?"

"At the school play last spring. But I could not know Lillian and not know Philippa. She was one of those rare people who generate . . . good feeling."

"Good feeling?" Mum raised her swallow-tailed brows and Miss Field actually looked away.

"Love," she amended sternly. "She generated love."

Mum closed her eyes and dropped her head in acknowledgment.

"Yes. You're right. There was no hate in her."

Miss Field went on to talk about the next school play and hoped Mum would come. She said matter-of-factly, "My house is very central, Mrs. Freeman. I would be happy to look after the baby if you and Lillian want to go out occasionally."

I had never discovered Miss Field's address. Even when I had wanted to send her a Christmas card in my second year, I had had to post it to the school.

She walked up to the road to meet Miss Crail and I went with her.

"Your mother does not know you are not attending school, Lillian," she said. "And I have no wish to worry her by mentioning it. However, the School Attendance officer will shortly call on you. You realize that."

"Yes."

We stood at the top of the track and stared toward Stroud. Miss Field's brogues looked as if they were growing out of the ground.

She said, "The only way to get over this, Lillian, is to fill your time. Work steadily through each day."

"It hardly seems worth it," I said dully. She waited and I tried to explain, though the effort was wearying. "If there was something to work for . . . or toward. There's nothing. Everything's gone."

"Your mother needs you."

"No!" I shook my head quickly brushing the words away before I could consider them. "She can manage. She's keeping going for the sake of the baby."

Miss Crail's car rounded the bend. Miss Field stooped and picked a snowdrop.

"You don't think you're wasting Philippa's love by not caring about anything?"

How could I begin to tell her the enormity of waste that had happened here? I just shook my head, not in negation but in a kind of dumb pain.

She handed me the snowdrop.

"Whether we wish it or not, Lillian, everything goes on. You cannot stop it. If you hang back or try to stand aside, it will run over you. It is inexorable."

How Phil would have loved to hear Miss Field use that word. How Phil would have loved that tiny snowdrop.

Mavis brought a friend home to tea. It was the first time since she'd arrived that she had been seen with another child. This one was the Willises' evacuee. Her name was Topaz, Pazzie for short. She never came out with Freda and I could see why immediately she entered the door. Freda's asthmatic whisper would have been drowned by Pazzie's strident announcements.

She told us as she came in, "Mam comes up when she's got some money and can put up with Mrs. Willis."

"No personal remarks please, Topaz. Take off your wet things and come by the fire." Mum pushed chairs into strategic positions.

"No. Well, I mean, Mam does come sometimes. Mavis' mam ain't been near her, has she?" I hung the two coats behind the door. Pazzie went on like an ever-rolling stream. "Coo, you gets looked after here, don't you?" She jerked her head at Mavis. "Course she don't say much, do she? But you can't expect her to like it. Her mam never writing nor nothing. She's a deep one, she is, if half what she been whispering to me is true —" Mavis tugged at her sleeve anxiously. "Oh. Ah. I was forgetting. Cross me 'eart and 'ope to die. Don't *worry* so, Mavis. You're all right with Pazzie."

Mavis giggled and Pazzie laughed raucously. Mum and I sat through tea and listened to tales of the Willises, and I began to feel a kind of nudging nostalgia to get together with Freda again and laugh as we used to. But it would never be possible to say all large-eyed and melodramatic, "*And* I hear your mum cuts the sausages down the middle lengthwise and *then* says you can only have half each for breakfast!" Impossible because of how Freda could retaliate. Pazzie had tales of Little Dorrit too, and the fruitless fight against lice in the vicarage. She

215

enacted the vicar preaching his sermon and scratching surreptitiously. It was the first time for ages Mum and me had laughed together.

They went upstairs afterward to share their secrets. I washed up and then went to collect Pazzie and take her home. They were sitting in the middle of the bed surrounded by bits of paper. Mavis was writing very carefully with a crayon.

"Making confetti?"

Mavis made a vain effort to gather the papers together with one arm. One piece fluttered to the floor. I picked it up. It said, "You are a hoar."

Pazzie started straight in. "It's a joke, see. We play it on the girls at school —"

I ignored her. "You wrote these, Mavis?"

"Pazzie did that one," Mavis said quickly.

"Hang about," squawked Pazzie. "I said I'd keep the secret. That's all. Not take the bleeding blame."

I said wonderingly, "You did them all. What a fool — why didn't I realize?"

Mavis darted in again. "Because you agreed with them — you probably wanted to do them yourself. I knew what it was like for you, Lil —"

"Mr. Edwards . . . as far back as that. My God." I stared at her blankly. "It was you. There was nothing to that. Nothing. That was why Freda knew nothing about it. There was nothing to know."

"He came here every Wednesday. There was talk —" Mavis protested.

"And he stopped coming. He stopped."

"They made him leave. Just like they tried to make your mum leave —"

"They gave him a white feather." I looked beyond Mavis, remembering. "They said nothing about Mum. They thought he was a coward. That was all."

Mavis scrabbled her papers up and stuffed them in her pillow case.

"She deserved it. You know she did. She's horrible. She thinks she's better 'n my mam. But she isn't. I heard about her having to get married. And now she's having another kid — it's horrible."

I walked to the door and opened it. Pazzie shot through.

"If it hadn't been for Mum, you'd be at the vicarage scratching like the others," I said heavily.

"It was you chose me. Not her. She never liked me — not from that first night when I shat in the bath." Mavis sobbed frantically. "Grandad and Phil . . . not her. Never her."

I looked back at her. She sat in the middle of her bed. Small and vicious. It was like looking at myself.

Pazzie said on the way back to the Willis cottage, "Now it's not a proper secret no more, I'd better tell you. She won't."

"What?" I prompted when even Pazzie dried up.

"She's sent one of those things — them letter things — to your dad."

"She doesn't know his address."

"She found a letter you'd had from him and throwed away."

I looked down at Gloucester and tried to imagine what Dad would do if he got an anonymous letter. He wouldn't do anything, would he? He was like me. He didn't care.

"I see."

I held open the Willises' gate. From the window Freda saw me and turned quickly away. I couldn't have been completely numb because that small gesture hurt.

Mum was taken to the hospital a week after that. Little Dorrit came across on her monumental bike each afternoon and made some sort of a meal for Mavis and me. It was a nuisance because I still had to pretend to go to school each day. On the other hand when the school inspector came, she told him about our "troubles" and he must have let my truancy go by for a while. I never heard any more about it.

Mr. Dorrit took me in to see Mum most evenings. If her blood pressure didn't return to normal, they were going to "bring the baby on." She said quietly, "Don't hate me, Lil. Please don't hate me anymore." And I said truthfully, "I don't hate you, Mum." It was something, surely?

Mr. Dorrit wanted us to go to the vicarage and Mavis was terrified of being in the house on our own. In the kitchen she whispered to me, "Could we be in the same room together, Lil?"

"I'm not going, Mavis. I can't leave home now."

She drooped. "Then I'll stay, too."

"For goodness' sake! You go. I don't mind —"

"No. I want to stay with you," she said stubbornly and with her queer loyalty.

That night I heard her shifting about and I got up and went in to her and sat with her till she fell asleep. It was what Phil had done so often. It was something else. Perhaps.

The next afternoon I was just considering clearing out of the house before Little Dorrit arrived when there was a scratching sound at the front door. I whipped into the hall and gazed paralyzed as it creaked and swung open slowly. Dad stood there.

He grinned at me. "Damn thing always was stiff," he said. He dropped a kit bag at his feet. "You've grown, Lil."

I'd imagined seeing him again. Being very cool and collected and taking hold of the situation. Now here he was. As tatty and familiar as our dear old GY. He'd married Mum because of me and I was his fetter until the war released him. Yet . . . he was my dad.

I made a moaning sound and felt my face sag and contract in a spasm.

"Lil . . . my chookie . . ." He opened his arms. "Come on, Lil."

We stood in the hall. Then we moved into the living room. When Little Dorrit arrived, he waved her away above my head. I heard her say, "I'm glad you're back, Mr. Freeman," then the door closed. I cried loudly, like a child, like Phil had cried. I

219

couldn't stop. Dad didn't try to make me stop. He rocked me. He propped me with cushions while he lit the fire I had laid this morning. He took me in his arms again, wiped my face and then his own. Mavis came in and went out again. When eventually, leaning exhaustedly against Dad's shoulder, I looked at the clock, it was five. I had cried for two hours.

Dad said in a low voice, "I could do with a cup of tea, Lil."

"Yes. Yes."

We went into the kitchen together and made a pot of tea. Dad fetched coal while I hacked bread and cheese. We sat down again. I felt light-headed, filled with enormous relief.

"Can you stay, Dad?" I glanced at him and altered that. "Will you stay?"

"If Mum will have me. If not, I'll doss down at Nanny Dexter's and come over each day."

I hadn't thought that Mum might not want Dad anymore.

I said, "How much do you know?"

"Enough. I had a letter . . . got compassionate leave. I went to see Flo and Bert, and they told me what they could. But I know the village better than they do. It must have been grim, Lily."

I shook my head. "It wasn't the village. It was us." I stared into the fire. "Mavis wrote the letters. And I could have done so much . . . but I didn't. I hated Mum." Tears ran again. "I don't anymore. Not since Phil died. I just hate myself."

"Ah Lil . . . poor chookie. My heritage to you. I've spent a lot of time hating myself. It's a complete waste of time, too. Worse than that, it pretty soon decays into being sorry for yourself."

I dashed at my eyes.

"I haven't been to school. I walk around and think of Phil —"

"If I'm coming home, you'll have to go to school. I never could stand kids around the house all day."

"What about . . . what about the new baby?"

"Ah, yes. I'll have to put up with that, won't I?"

I blew my nose and looked at him. "Won't you mind, Dad?"

"Mind? Don't be an idiot, Lil. I'll mind like hell. But if I go away and never see you or Mum again, I'll mind a damned sight worse. I'll have to get used to . . . it. That's all."

"I wish I could be like that. Miss Field told me I had to accept it. But I'm so tired, Dad. I don't seem to care."

"Go to sleep now, then. Right here in front of the fire. I'll visit Mum tonight and we'll sort something out."

He got off the sofa and pushed me down into the cushions. It was warm and I was relaxed. He covered me with his greatcoat and leaned over me, looking at my face intently.

I said, "Dad . . . do you think . . . now . . . that you know what love is?"

My eyes were heavy and half closed but I saw that he remembered his own words. He shook his head.

"I don't know, Lil. I've discovered that I don't want to live without you, chookie. Is that love?"

"Are there lights? All around the house? Shining —"

"You and Mum both were haloes, my darling."

I smiled, satisfied. "That's it, Dad. That's it." I touched the rough cloth of his uniform and was reminded of Bob's Harris tweed jacket and the light glancing off laurel leaves and stones. Like Ron said, it was still there. But you needed to stand back from it to see it properly.

That night Bob and Mum's baby was born. It was a boy. Dad stayed with her all the time, and Little Dorrit slept at our house and took us to Stroud the next day.

Mum looked fine; there was no sign of the baby.

"He's in the nursery." She sounded so ... normal. "He's fair, six and a half pounds, about five weeks premature but very strong and healthy."

Dad looked awful. He said expressionlessly, "You sound proud of yourself."

She looked at us both in turn. Her dark eyes were not defiant or hurt. She said quietly, "I am. I'm not apologizing anymore, my dears. I've caused you both unhappiness, I know that, but I'm going to work hard to put that right. This baby ... he's a miracle. I love him."

Dad caught her hand. "Well done, Grace. Well done. Every time I speak out of turn, tell me where to get off —"

"I always did, Albert." She smiled.

"No. You pecked at me. You tried to needle me back. Someone has to say — stop —"

"Phil always did that," I put in. "She absorbed things. Earthed nasty things. Like a lightning conductor."

"Let's try to be like Phil." Mum smiled all around. Then she asked about the house and the chickens and whether we had enough coal for a fire all day and what were Little Dorrit's meals like.

Then she said, "Now. Lily, my dear — go and look at Henry."

"Henry?"

"It was Grandad's name. Dad and I chose it last night."

I was thankful she wasn't calling him Robert. But I still didn't want to see him. I trailed along to the nursery and looked at the names clipped onto the canvas cots with clothes-pegs. There were only two babies there anyway, and I'd have known ours anywhere. Ours . . . it came so naturally as I looked at him.

I leaned over him. I had steeled myself against him looking like Bob. I had hoped there might be a look of Phil about him. But — even to my eyes — he was like me. It was natural, I suppose; Bob's fairness and Mum's darkness had combined to produce another mousey child, but it was more than coloring. His forehead bulged, his eyes were a bit too deep set, his chin was thrust out. Bob had given me something after all. A brother.

I knelt by the cot for a long time. I knew what was happening to me and I didn't want it to stop or be interrupted. The vacuum was being filled. Love was coming back.

Dad came behind me, lifted me, and held me propped against him.

He said in a low voice, "D'you think we can put up with him, Lil?"

"I can. Can you?"

"He's Mum's. And he's yours. That's enough reason."

I whispered, "You'll be all right, Henry. You've got a family and you've got the hills. You'll be all right." It was what Bob would have wanted for his son, too. And what Phil had given to her small, new cousin.

CHAPTER
NINETEEN

Ron said, "They're having a bonfire at Gloucester Cross tonight. Burning an effigy of old Hitler. Are you going?"

"No." I adjusted my satchel on my shoulder. It weighed a ton. I was in the middle of my school Certificate. "Little Dorrit asked us to help with the evacuees' home-going party. And Dad's on early turn. We go to bed by ten."

"You'll probably be able to see it from your window, anyway. Seems funny. The war over."

"No one to blame for everything that goes wrong?" I grinned at him ruefully. "We'd have still had our war without old Hitler, Ron."

"A different one, though. No Bob Critchley. No Phil living with you. Would you have wanted to miss that?"

"No." I could answer steadily now. Henry was over a year old; beginning to walk, fat and cuddly with a delightful chuckle that could make Dad laugh even on night turn. Because of him, I could stand back and look at what happened, marvel over it, just as Ron had said.

"Quite honestly, Ron, all the yelling and shouting seem daft. The only thing I'm pleased about is that poor old Mavis is going back home."

"And no one else is being killed or wounded?" he prompted.

"Yes. Of course, yes."

He stopped short. His satchel slipped to the ground. "Hey — look, Lil. There's smoke coming out of Nanny Dexter's chimney! She must be better." He swung his satchel. "Just in time for V-E Day — good old Nan!"

Nan had lived through the last year in spite of herself. Freda, Ron, and I had taken her a meal each evening; Mrs. Crake had replenished her store of bottled fruit.

I said tentatively, "You're in good spirits, Ron. And we've come home with Mr. Willis, too!" Miss Crail was away from school with a summer cold.

He started to slither down the summer grass toward Nan's cottage.

"That's it, Lil. I've been almost certain all winter. Today confirmed it. I'm free. I'm free again, Lil!"

I watched him gallop down the steep slope in giant strides, whooping like he used to, slapping the sides of an imaginary horse. The war was over. Had it really been a forcing-house, a greenhouse, for growing up? Or would it have been exactly the same without old Hitler and his Merry Men? And could we go back to being children again? Not like we'd been before . . . but still children?

226

Ron reached the pond and yelled back, "Come on — let's go and see Nan and then we can take Henry for a paddle in the stream before tea."

Ron was coming to tea. He often did.

I tried to follow him sedately.

"Ron, we're nearly seventeen. We can't still paddle in the brook. Freda says we still act like kids and we're immature in some ways."

Ron said a very rude word, and I giggled and pelted down the last few yards to join him.

Nan had a bottle of elderberry wine on the table and three mugs.

"I knew you'd come. It was in the leaves," she said incorrigibly. "So . . . it's over, m'dears. We'll drink a toast. Come on. Sit you down. You're both so tall I can hardly see you against the light."

"What'll we drink to, Nan?" Ron asked, gloating over his mug. "Peace and Prosperity?"

"Now you two both know we'll never have that." Nan lifted her mug. Her hat was fair and square on her knob of hair, flames flickered in her grate, pale against the sunshine. "We'll drink to Philippa, m'dears. And we'll drink to a land where people like our Phil can live and be free."

We lifted our mugs and clanked them together.

It was, after all, everything we could possibly want. A land where people like my cousin could live and be free.

To Phil . . .

ISIS publish a wide range of books in large print, from fiction to biography. Any suggestions for books you would like to see in large print or audio are always welcome. Please send to the Editorial Department at:

ISIS Publishing Ltd.
7 Centremead
Osney Mead
Oxford OX2 0ES
(01865) 250 333

A full list of titles is available free of charge from:
Ulverscroft Large Print Books

(UK)
The Green
Bradgate Road, Anstey
Leicester LE7 7FU
Tel: (0116) 236 4325

(Australia)
P.O Box 953
Crows Nest
NSW 1585
Tel: (02) 9436 2622

(USA)
1881 Ridge Road
P.O Box 1230, West Seneca,
N.Y. 14224-1230
Tel: (716) 674 4270

(Canada)
P.O Box 80038
Burlington
Ontario L7L 6B1
Tel: (905) 637 8734

(New Zealand)
P.O Box 456
Feilding
Tel: (06) 323 6828

Details of **ISIS** complete and unabridged audio books are also available from these offices. Alternatively, contact your local library for details of their collection of **ISIS** large print and unabridged audio books.